What the opposing sexes say about marriage:

He Says: "Marriage? Forget it. I'll *never* consider marrying another woman ever again—one broken engagement's enough, thank you very much. No, I enjoy my bachelor life too much to get serious about anyone. Of course, my *very* attractive next-door neighbor has been causing me some sleepless nights—no, just friends, that's all I'm looking for...."

—Britt Carlton, 31

She Says: "*Marriage?!* I'm taking a break from *dating* for the rest of my life. I'm young, I'm attractive...I'm stupid. After all, *I* was the last to know that my fiancé was the Womanizer of Wichita! Anyway, I'm not bitter, I just want to start a new life...with new friends. Speaking of friends, there's this handsome charmer who lives next door. He could be fun to hang out with—on a strictly platonic level, of course...."

—Ashley Thornton, 25

You'll Say: "Just friends? Yeah, right...."

Dear Reader,

"Just friends." When you're talking men and women, those two words can mean exactly what they say, or they can hide a wealth of attraction underneath their bland exterior. I happen to be friends—*just* friends—with a couple of guys. They're great. They give me a whole different perspective on things like movies, and I can even go to them for interpretations of the male psyche when I have a date with a guy who seems to have come from an entirely different planet. But speaking of entirely different…that's the way to interpret "just friends" when you're talking about the hero and heroine of Shawna Delacorte's *Much Ado About Marriage.* They start out planning to keep things platonic, but…well, let's just say they don't succeed, and that what *does* happen is a whole lot more fun.

There's also fun in store in Linda Lewis's *Cinderella and the Texas Prince.* Seems there's a bit of competition going on at Travis Rule's ranch. The bride candidates are in residence— and in trouble. Because the unlikeliest woman of all seems to have the lead when it comes to winning the heart of the richest bachelor in Texas. Miss Cindy Ellerbee—the *housekeeper,* for heaven's sake!—is cooking and cleaning and *kissing* those other women right out of Travis's mind. Seems as if there's a Western wedding on the way.

Have fun with both these great books, and don't forget to come back next month for two more wonderful novels all about meeting—and marrying—Mr. Right.

Enjoy!

Leslie Wainger
Senior Editor and Editorial Coordinator

Please address questions and book requests to:
Silhouette Reader Service
U.S.: 3010 Walden Ave., P.O. Box 1325, Buffalo, NY 14269
Canadian: P.O. Box 609, Fort Erie, Ont. L2A 5X3

SHAWNA DELACORTE

Much Ado About Marriage

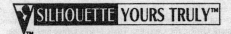

SILHOUETTE YOURS TRULY™

Published by Silhouette Books ·
America's Publisher of Contemporary Romance

I would like to extend a special thank-you to John for providing me with enough technical information to ditch a small airplane in the ocean...and live to tell about it.

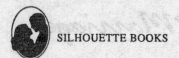 SILHOUETTE BOOKS

ISBN 0-373-52069-7

MUCH ADO ABOUT MARRIAGE

About the author

Thank you for purchasing this copy of
Much Ado About Marriage. Ashley and Britt were
fun characters to work with and I hope you enjoy
reading their story as much as I did writing it.

Much Ado About Marriage is set primarily in
Seattle, Washington. Even though I've lived most of
my life in the Los Angeles area, many of my books
have been set in the Pacific Northwest. It is my
favorite part of the country, and I visit there as
often as possible. I hope to be able to move to the
Seattle area in the not-too-distant future.

For many years I made my living in the
entertainment industry as a television production
manager. Four years ago I finally took that
frightening step known as "quitting the day job" to
concentrate on writing full-time. My hobbies are
travel and photography.

I am always interested in hearing from my readers.
I can be reached at 6505 E. Central, Box 300,
Wichita, KS 67206.

Enjoy!

Shawna Delacorte

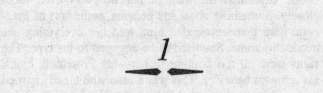

1

"Hey! What's with all the racket?" The angry tone matched the disagreeable utterance. "Is it absolutely necessary for you to be banging on my wall?"

The sound startled Ashley Thornton. She jerked her head in the direction the voice came from and saw its very masculine owner framed in her opened front door. The stranger's voice projected a combination of perfected smoothness and a hint of the thickness associated with someone who'd just woken up.

Her appraisal took in a man a little over six feet tall with broad shoulders and long legs. No question about it—he possessed the type of good looks that could easily turn any woman's head. As she scrutinized him more closely, she noted his tousled sandy blond hair and at least a day's growth of beard, further evidence that he'd probably just woken up.

"I'm sorry." Her tone conveyed a bit of an edge as she leaned the picture against the wall, set the hammer on the table and glanced at her watch. Four o'clock in the afternoon did not seem like a time when a little noise should be as bothersome as this grumpy, though good-looking, man professed. "I didn't realize I was disturbing anyone. I was trying to hang some pictures." For some inexplicable reason she felt the need to add, "I've just moved in,'' as if the jumble of boxes strewn around the studio apartment did not speak for themselves.

She examined the man in her doorway even more closely. Something about his persona, some sort of magnetic aura that surrounded him, told her everything she needed to know. She used to be engaged to his type. The signs were all too familiar to her—his irresistible looks, his arrogant behavior. This was a man who clearly partied too much and who probably had a string of casual affairs, one-night stands and simultaneous girlfriends to his credit. Or, more accurately, to his *discredit.*

She noticed the way his gaze darted around the room. He seemed to be searching for something, but she wasn't sure what.

Britt Carlton surveyed the scene, carefully taking in everything. His anger softened considerably. He had only gotten to sleep four hours earlier and his head felt as large as a watermelon, neither of which were this woman's fault. If only he had been scheduled for a flight, he could have begged off from attending the bachelor party. Besides, bachelor parties reminded him of weddings. A shudder ran through his body at the memory of his own near nuptials. Now that was a lesson he had learned the hard way, but a lesson that had stuck. As far as he was concerned, marriage was a thoroughly repugnant topic to be avoided if at all possible.

''So I see.'' His expression softened and then he flashed the most dazzling smile Ashley had ever seen. ''I didn't mean to yell. You woke me from some much-needed sleep.''

''Oh?'' She crossed the room toward him. ''Do you work nights?'' Her first impulse was to make a caustic comment about it not being her fault that he had been out carousing all night, but she thought better of it. There was no reason to create an awkward scene with a neighbor before she even settled into her new apartment.

"No, just a bad night that lasted too long." He extended his hand toward her. "I'm Britt Carlton, your next-door neighbor." He cocked his head to one side, indicating the direction of his apartment. "Welcome to the building."

"Thank you. I'm Ashley Thornton." The warmth of his touch tingled her senses as they shook hands. He was even better looking up close. His silver eyes, though slightly bloodshot, sparkled as he smiled—a smile that seemed to come easy to his sensuous mouth, blending perfectly with his handsome features.

She stepped back from the front door. "Excuse my lack of manners." Even if he had been tactless in chastising her unjustly, she would show him she was above it. "Please, come in." She picked up a box from a chair in order to make a place for him to sit.

"Here, let me get that for you." He took the box from her and set it on the floor as his gaze slowly drifted over her.

Britt Carlton had had lots of practice in sizing up women. He immediately pegged her height as five foot six, and he'd already noticed the fluid way she walked. He settled his attention on her face. Her eyes totally captivated him. They were the most incredible turquoise color he had ever seen and were rimmed by the longest, darkest lashes.

He looked around the room at all the cartons. "Would you like some help? Tote that barge, lift that bale…" He glanced toward the campaign couch that doubled as a bed—the brass back and side railings polished to a high gloss, the couch back cushions resting on the floor—and gave her a mischievous grin and a wink. "I'd be happy to help you make up the bed."

She tried to suppress a grin, but did not quite make it. His glib comments, charming manner and subtle innuendoes seemed to come easily to him. Yet more evidence of the womanizer she suspected him of being. The corners of her mouth turned up slightly. "You're much too kind, and I can't begin to tell you how much I appreciate your generous offer, but I think I can manage that one by myself."

"Never let it be said that I neglected my gentlemanly duties by not offering to help a lady in distress."

"That vicious rumor will never escape these lips."

His gaze dropped from her eyes to her mouth. Her pink lips were slightly parted, tantalizingly curled upward at the corners and much too tempting. He felt the tightness across his chest. It was a mouth that simply begged to be kissed. He tried to project a casual outer manner, even though it was a far cry from what was going on inside him. "Exactly what would escape those lips?"

Her gaze flew to his mouth, the teasing grin that widened into a dazzling smile then slowly faded as he leaned slightly forward. Was he going to try to kiss her? A tremor darted across her nape. She wanted to believe that it was an adverse reaction to her thought, but it felt more like anticipation. She took a quick step backward in an attempt to put a little physical distance between them. She did not know how to respond to his question. Intellectually she wanted to dismiss it, but emotionally she wanted to embrace the unexpected desire it had produced.

Britt immediately recognized the discomfort his question had caused. He had not meant to put her on the spot like that. He made the first move to end it.

"You obviously have a lot to do, so I won't keep you

any longer.'' He hesitated for a moment. His manner softened and his voice clearly conveyed his embarrassment. ''I'm sorry I got all bent out of shape about the noise.'' He looked around the room. ''Are you sure you don't need any help?'' He smiled reassuringly. ''It's a sincere offer.''

''Thanks, I appreciate it. But I think I'm just going to unpack some of my basic necessities and tackle the rest of this mess first thing in the morning.'' She brushed a loose tendril of hair away from her face and rubbed at what she knew was a dirty smudge on her cheek. ''When I'm fresh and rested,'' she added.

She held out her hand toward him. ''Well, it's certainly been interesting meeting you.''

His dazzling smile lit up his face as he shook her hand. ''I insist on taking that as a compliment, no matter how you really intended it.''

He was a smooth one, all right. She pitied any woman who actually dated him in good faith, assuming that it could in any way lead to a meaningful relationship. Putting on an elaborate display of hurt, she spoke in a teasing tone of voice. ''Are you doubting my veracity? I don't think you know me well enough to be doing that.''

''That's a problem easily solved.'' He flashed a grin, then teasingly whispered, ''Exactly what do I need to do to become familiar with your illusive veracity?'' His expression abruptly turned serious. ''What about my simply getting to know you better? Why don't we start there and see where it takes us?''

She cocked her head and tried to suppress a little grin. ''Are you certain you want to know me better? You might be disappointed.''

''Time will tell!'' He gave her a quick wink. ''Good afternoon, Ashley. It's been a real pleasure.'' He shot her a comical leer and headed for the door. "Try to keep the noise down. I need my rest if I'm going to keep up my strength and stamina." With that, he left her apartment, closing the door behind him.

Ashley walked out onto her balcony, the cool breeze from Elliott Bay tickling several strands of her dark hair against her cheek. Britt Carlton was a totally outrageous man. She unconsciously shook her head as the smile left her lips. Yep, she knew his type all too well. Enjoy the laughs and the fun but do not, under any circumstances, get involved emotionally with someone like that. There was no future with a man like Britt Carlton, and anyone who thought there was would only end up being hurt. She knew from experience what it was like to be engaged to someone like that. It could only lead to heartbreak.

Upon returning to his apartment, Britt was shocked to find three people sitting in his living room. He hid the irritation that immediately grabbed at him. His head still pounded. He was not accustomed to drinking very much, and he had overdone it at the bachelor party. All he wanted was to go back to bed and get some much-needed sleep. But no one seemed to be cooperating.

Darlene and Bob lived in the apartment directly above his and knew he never locked the door when he was still somewhere in the apartment complex. So it was not unusual for them to barge in unannounced. But the third person...he didn't know the woman with them, however he did know the type.

She tried too hard to look sexy, to act alluring, to present herself as an irresistible package. He was sure it probably worked for her elsewhere, but it left him cold. His gaze fell on Darlene and Bob. This could only be yet another of Darlene's endless matchmaking attempts. He gathered as much of his practiced charm as he could muster and hid his annoyance behind a smiling facade. "Aren't you going to introduce me to your lovely friend?"

Darlene's voice bubbled with enthusiasm. "This is my cousin from Phoenix, Julie Robertson. Julie, this is the man we were telling you about—Britt Carlton."

"Julie, it's a pleasure to meet you. Is this your first trip to Seattle?"

"Oh, my, no." Julie spoke with a forced breathiness that she apparently thought sounded sexy. She extended her hand to Britt, her manner indicating that she expected him to kiss the back of it while giving some sort of courtly bow. "I've visited Darlene and Bob before. I just adore Seattle." She waved her other hand in an exaggerated gesture that seemed to encompass the surrounding area and all the greater outdoors. "Everything is so green and there's water just everywhere."

He ignored the phoniness of her actions, shook her hand firmly, then let go of it. "Yes, Seattle is a very pretty city. How long will you be in town?"

"I plan to stay for two weeks, unless..." She let her voice trail off as she blatantly admired him. "Unless something happens to alter my plans."

He flashed her one of his best smiles, his outward manner giving no hint of his inner thoughts. "Good hunting!"

Darlene quickly jumped into the conversation. "Why don't you have dinner with us tomorrow night? Bob is cooking, so it will probably be edible." Darlene and Bob both laughed while Britt rolled his eyes upward in mock dismay. The last time he'd had dinner with them Darlene had burned the roast, serving something that tasted more like charcoal than meat.

"I'd love to, but unfortunately I'm on standby to fly a charter tomorrow night. I'll have to take a rain check."

"Fair enough. Well, we have to be going or we'll be late for the movie," Bob said as he and Darlene started for the front door.

Julie slowly unwound herself from the end of the couch and seductively moved to Britt's side. She placed her hand against his chest, looked up at his face and pursed her mouth in a highly perfected half pout, half pucker with her wet lips slightly parted. She pressed her body against his. "Would you like to go to the movies with us? We could share some popcorn during the movie…and so much more afterward."

Britt flashed her a practiced smile. "It sounds real tempting. Unfortunately, I already have plans for this evening." He heard her whimper of disappointment, then watched as she made a little kissing motion with her lips as she turned toward the door. He watched as the three of them left his apartment.

Britt wiped the smile from his face as soon as the door clicked shut. He expelled a long breath and muttered his irritation out loud. "I wish to hell Darlene would stop trying to fix me up with every single woman she knows."

He strolled into the kitchen, opened the freezer door and removed a nearly empty carton of his favorite chocolate fudge mousse ice cream. He grabbed a spoon from the drawer, then headed for the living room to watch the five o'clock evening news.

As he leaned back on the couch with his long legs stretched out in front of him, his thoughts turned to Ashley. No matter how hard he tried, he could not get the image of her incredible turquoise eyes out of his mind. He finished the last bite of ice cream, then rinsed the carton and threw it away. He poured himself a glass of milk, then settled back into the couch to watch the weather report.

But Britt didn't feel settled. He still felt guilty about the way he had barged into Ashley's apartment and the rude manner in which he had complained about the noise. Hanging pictures at four o'clock in the afternoon was a perfectly acceptable activity. His outburst had been totally out of line. He knew it had been more than the throbbing headache that caused his bad mood. For the past week he had been trying to fight off the flu, none too successfully.

He reflected again on the brief time he had spent with Ashley. He'd felt very relaxed, considering the incessant pounding behind his eyes and across his temples. He did not like uptight women who had no sense of humor, but she had gone along with him and did not seem uncomfortable with his teasing.

He also felt a little guilty about telling Darlene and Bob he was on standby for a charter flight, but he had no interest in spending an evening with someone like Julie. Without being egotistical about it, Britt knew the impact his good looks had on women. There were certainly enough of them throwing themselves at him, and he was more than happy to take some of them up on their offers.

A slight frown wrinkled his forehead. At least that was how he'd felt up until about six months ago when it had finally hit him that he had been living a very shallow life without emotional involvement. He dismissed the uncomfortable thoughts from his mind, preferring to turn his attention to the program on television.

Following Britt's departure from her apartment, Ashley finished unpacking clothes then decided to call it a day. After filling the tub, she settled herself in the hot bubble bath, the jasmine scented water soothing her tired aching muscles. As she relaxed, her thoughts turned to the events that had culminated with her move to Seattle and what she hoped would be the start of a new life.

The previous six months had been an emotional roller coaster for her. The man she had been engaged to, Jerry Broderick, had managed to find time to date two other women while betrothed to her. The charming manner, the easy flattery, the glib conversation, the handsome features and piercing eyes, the dazzling smile, the sexy laugh, the string of meaningless compliments—oh, yes, she knew it all too well. The Jerry Brodericks and the Britt Carltons of the world were cut from the same cloth. Britt's blond good looks and silver eyes might be in direct contrast to Jerry's dark hair and eyes, but the manner was the same. She had been taken in by a lothario once. She would not be taken in again.

Even after she had broken the engagement and returned his ring, Jerry continued to profess his undying love. She had told him, as honestly and as straightforward as possible, that their relationship was over. He had refused to listen, telling her she was being unreasonable about an unimportant little transgression—after all, he was a man and things were *different* with men.

A twinge of anger jabbed at her when she recalled his words. Any hope that might have existed for a reconciliation had been destroyed the moment he tried to impose his double standard of behavior on her.

Philosophically she accepted the broken engagement as a sign to break new ground and make some changes in her life. The first change had involved moving from her hometown of Wichita, Kansas. The decision had not been an easy one. She hated to leave her family, but she wanted to experience new things, meet new challenges and enjoy whatever new experiences life had to offer. Her parents and brother understood and supported her decision.

She had procured a good position as administrative assistant to Stuart Billington, President of The Billington Group, a prominent Seattle corporation. The new job did not start for another three weeks yet. She was delighted to have the extra time to settle in, explore her new city and acclimate herself.

The warm bathwater, she realized, was doing its job of soothing her sore muscles and allowing her to relax. Her thoughts began to drift as her eyelids grew heavy. Somewhere in the back of her mind lurked a mental image of Britt Carlton's handsomely chiseled features.

Ashley's eyes snapped open and her body stiffened to attention. His unexpected intrusion into her thoughts both disturbed and concerned her. It was not an image she wanted to carry to bed with her, regardless of how tantalizing she found the idea.

Britt stood on his balcony, sipping his coffee and watching the rain that obscured the morning sky. The cold damp air caused a shiver to move up his spine. He returned to the kitchen and poured himself some more coffee, then impulsively grabbed a second mug, filled it with coffee and hurried out the front door of his apartment.

Ashley had just finished running a brush through her hair and putting on a touch of lipstick when she heard the doorbell. She opened the door to be greeted by a mug of steaming coffee thrust into her hands.

"I hope you drink it black." Britt flashed a dazzling smile as he walked into her apartment without waiting to be invited. He paused a moment, his expression turning serious. "Listen…about yesterday. I just want to apologize again. I'm sorry I behaved like an—"

"Don't worry about it." She offered him an engaging smile. "The entire incident is forgotten. Are you feeling better today? Caught up on your sleep?"

"Much better, thanks." He casually perched on the edge of her unmade bed, stretched his long legs out in front of him, and leaned back against the brass railing. He took a sip of his coffee while trying to ignore the stuffiness that threatened to hamper his breathing.

His gaze wandered over her appearance. She had pulled her hair back from her face, a gold clasp holding it at her nape. A bit of color dotted her lips. She wore jeans, a man's football jersey and socks without shoes. He entertained a brief thought as to whether the jersey belonged to her boyfriend. "So this is what you look like when you're clean and rested."

She felt a slight flush spread across her cheeks. "I was a bit of a mess yesterday, wasn't I?" She took a sip from the mug. "Thanks for the coffee. This really hits the spot. I haven't unpacked a thing in the kitchen yet. I'm not even sure where the coffeepot is."

He looked rested, too. His silver eyes sparkled, his thick blond hair appeared casual yet carefully groomed and he was clean shaven. He wore faded jeans and across the front of his long-sleeved T-shirt was printed, "If God had intended man to fly, he would have given him airplane tickets."

"Does this have any particular significance?" She touched the wording on his shirt. Her fingers lingered for just a moment as she became aware of the hardness of his body, his firm muscle tone.

He arched an eyebrow as he watched her delicate fingers move against his chest. "Actually, yes. It was a birthday present from my sister. She said she couldn't think of anything more appropriate to give to a pilot."

"Is that what you do for a living?"

"That's it. I fly charters, mostly for corporate executives." He noted the creamy smooth texture of her skin, the rich lustrous quality of her dark brown hair and those incredible eyes again—large expressive turquoise eyes surrounded by the longest dark lashes. The sensation of her touch lingered with him even though she had long since withdrawn her hand. He shoved away the sensation and quickly rose to his feet.

He ambled toward the kitchen as he spoke. "I'll give you a hand with the unpacking. You tell me what to do and I'll do it."

"I'll gratefully accept any help I can get!"

He stopped, spun around and raised his eyebrows in a questioning expression as he cocked his head. "Oh? And just how grateful would that be?" His impish grin quickly dispelled any discomfort his suggestive words and tone of voice might have caused.

"I'd say just about grateful enough to spring for an inexpensive lunch when we've finished."

His grin widened into a dazzling smile. "You're on! Let's get to work."

For the next five hours they unpacked boxes, put things away and carried out trash. As soon as she restored the bed to a couch and replaced the last of the couch back pillows, Britt plopped down on it. He leaned back in the corner, his arms stretched along the top of the brass railings, and grinned at her.

"And they say a woman's work is never done, but as you can see when a *man* does it..." He allowed his voice to trail off as he eyed her curiously, waiting to see her reaction to his teasing comment.

She grabbed one of the couch pillows and playfully threw it at him. "Just for that, you can pay for lunch!"

He ducked and chuckled as he rose from the couch. "Well if I must, then I must. Shall we go?"

"Whoa! I need to clean up and change clothes first."

"No problem. Why don't you come on over to my place when you're ready." He glanced down at his own clothes. "It probably wouldn't hurt if I changed clothes, too." He reached out and gave her hand a quick squeeze. "I'll see you in a bit," he said, then quickly retreated to his apartment.

Britt kicked off his shoes, removed his jeans and T-shirt and tossed them on his bed, then took a quick shower. Afterward he pulled on a clean pair of jeans, then grabbed a sweater from the dresser drawer and carried it with him as he hurried to answer the doorbell.

"Ooooh, that's the way I like a man to answer his door." Julie purred seductively as she ran her hand across his bare chest, ruffling her fingers through the feathery wisps of sandy colored hair.

"Julie...this is a surprise." He hadn't given her a thought since she left his apartment the previous afternoon. A sharp jab of irritation shot through his body. He had hoped he wouldn't be seeing her again.

"A pleasant one, I hope." She trailed her fingers across his chest again, then over his shoulder as she brushed past him into his entry hall.

He clenched, then unclenched his jaw as he maintained his position at the opened doorway. "I was just getting ready to leave. Is there something I can do for you?"

She retraced her steps to where he waited by the door. She ran her fingers across the back of his neck. "I'll bet there's lots of things you can do for me—starting with this." She pressed her body against his, pulled his head down to her mouth and flicked her tongue across his lower lip.

He quickly jerked his head away from her and took a step back, bumping into the wall behind him. He looked up just in time to see Ashley. She shot him a scathing look that clearly telegraphed her disgust at what she had seen. Without saying a word, she turned on her heel and disappeared around the corner of the building.

Britt managed to extricate himself from Julie's clutches without being too rude or abrasive. "You'll have to excuse me, I was just leaving and I'm running late."

Julie reluctantly stepped back, pausing to run her fingers across his taut chest again. She slowly ran the tip of her tongue across her upper lip before speaking. "Well, I guess I'll be running along then." Her gaze lingered on his bare chest. "At least for now." She made an elaborate show of pursing her lips in a silent kiss before leaving.

Britt clenched his jaw in anger as he watched Julie climb the stairs toward Bob and Darlene's apartment. He had not made a good first impression with Ashley. First, he had yelled at her about making too much noise. Then, when he'd tried to smooth it over with her by taking her to lunch, she walked around the corner and right into the middle of that ludicrous scene. He pulled his sweater over his head, grabbed his hooded rain jacket from the closet and headed next door to Ashley's apartment.

A pang of disappointment mixed with the resentment and anger that was already churning in Ashley's stomach. Her first impression of Britt Carlton had been correct—he was an unabashed womanizer, just like Jerry Broderick. He had been expecting her, knew she would be at his apartment any minute, but he'd still managed a quick tryst without even bothering to close the door.

She tried to soothe her ruffled feathers with the thought that it did not really matter. She barely knew Britt Carlton.

They had no personal relationship, so his activities with other women were hardly any of her business. She wrinkled her brow into a frown and scrunched up her mouth. She did allow that it was the woman who'd seemed to be the aggressor rather than the other way around. In all fairness she also had to admit that Britt seemed somewhat taken aback by the woman's actions. She could even say he appeared genuinely startled.

She was doing it again, and after she had learned such a valuable lesson from her ex-fiancé. She had actually started to rationalize his actions, to make excuses for his blatantly womanizing ways. She clenched her jaw in determination as she silently renewed her vow *never* to fall for that type of man again. It could only lead to disaster.

2

A slight twinge of nervousness settled in the bottom of
Britt's stomach when Ashley opened her front door. Her
expression said she was displeased, but her eyes told him
there was more behind her attitude than what was apparent on the surface. He quickly offered his explanation before she had a chance to say anything.

"Her name's Julie and she's visiting Bob and Darlene,
who live upstairs. She's Darlene's cousin. I just met her
last night. She's, uh, shall we say...overly aggressive.
When I heard the doorbell, I thought it was you. She
barged in as soon as I opened the door without even being
invited."

Ashley tried for a nonchalant tone, but her voice had a
cold edge to it as she tried to dismiss the incident as if it
had no meaning. "You certainly don't owe me any ex-
planations. Your private life isn't any of my business."
As she looked at Britt's earnest expression, her attitude
softened. Despite the fact that she was sure she had him
pegged, knew exactly who and what he was, she still
found him interesting and fun. She reluctantly conceded
the fact that he seemed genuinely embarrassed about the
entire incident.

She flashed him a teasing grin, deciding it would serve
no purpose to remain angry. She would simply let the

incident pass. "Perhaps I should have stayed and rescued you from that assault on your person." She gave him a wry look and paraphrased his own words from the day before. "Never let it be said that I neglected my ladylike duties by not offering to help a gentleman in distress."

"That vicious rumor will never escape these lips," he said, teasing her with her own retort. He breathed a sigh of relief that the awkwardness of the situation had passed. Slowly the grin faded from his face as he looked into her eyes, then allowed his gaze to drop to her mouth—that lush, delicious-looking mouth that still begged to be kissed.

Her pulse rate increased slightly. She took an involuntary step back as a quick tremor shot through her body. Things were getting a little too hot and heavy for the circumstances. Fun and laughs were one thing, but hadn't she already been burned by a man not unlike Britt?

She ran her hand through her hair as the full impact of her words dawned on her. "Well." She nervously cleared her throat. "I believe we covered that yesterday." She hoped he did not catch her flustered condition. "Now, if I recall correctly, you were going to buy me lunch."

"Right you are. Is there anywhere special you'd like to eat?"

"Being new to Seattle, I'll have to leave that to your discretion."

"Oh? I didn't realize you'd moved to this apartment complex from out of town. Where are you from?"

"Wichita, Kansas. Have you ever been there?"

"Actually, I have. Several aircraft manufacturers are located there. I've picked up airplanes direct from the factory on many occasions and ferried them back here." They walked along together toward the parking garage. "What brings you from Wichita to Seattle?"

"A new job, new surroundings…a little change in my life."

Britt and Ashley enjoyed a leisurely late lunch, alternately laughing and talking seriously. All concerns and embarrassment over the earlier situation seemed to have been completely vanquished. She told him about her family in Wichita. That her mother worked as a legal secretary and her father was general manager of a radio station. Her younger brother was a senior in college and on a football scholarship. She did not bother to mention her broken engagement, deciding it was not relevant, but she did tell him about her new job.

"You're going to work for The Billington Group? Stu Billington is one of my best clients. I'm always flying him somewhere." Britt grinned at her. "Small world, isn't it?"

Britt went on to talk about flying. He'd started flying at the age of thirteen, knowing even then that it was the only thing he ever really wanted to do. Even so, he had earned his degree in business administration. His father had spent thirty years as an airline pilot and was now retired and living with Britt's mom in Florida. Britt also had a sister who was married and lived in Dallas. It didn't escape Ashley's notice that *he* did not talk about any past relationships, either.

"Brittlow Pennington Carlton," she said, "that's quite a mouthful."

"Brittlow is my mother's maiden name, and Pennington is my paternal grandmother's maiden name. My folks wanted to cover all bases." He grinned mischievously, followed by a quick wink. "You can never tell where an inheritance might be lurking."

By the time they returned to the apartment complex,

both of them felt as if they had known each other for a long time rather than just two days. There was no pressure or awkwardness between them, only an easy camaraderie. Neither of them considered the afternoon to be part of the excruciatingly complex dating game—jockeying for position, attempting to hold the advantage, trying to impress each other with superficialities and exaggerations. No, that certainly hadn't been the case and when Britt left her at her front door, he'd bestowed an innocent little kiss on her cheek.

Alone in her new apartment, Ashley plopped down on her couch, grabbed the remote for the television and flipped on the local news. Britt had promised to take her sight-seeing the next morning. A slight frown wrinkled her brow. Sight-seeing was not really a date, she reasoned. Besides, she had no objections to being *friends* with him—after all, he was a lot of fun—but she certainly was not interested in actually dating Britt Carlton. She quickly dismissed the concern. She knew better than to become emotionally involved with someone like Britt Carlton.

She did find her current situation unusual and interesting, though. She had never had a male friend to hang out with—someone who was just a buddy without the pressure of an intimate, committed relationship. She allowed an inward smile to make its way to the corners of her mouth. It was a nice feeling. She decided she was glad Britt lived next door to her. She turned her thoughts to the next day's sight-seeing. She hoped it wouldn't rain.

Britt stared up at the bedroom ceiling as he lay in bed. It was nearly midnight and he was still wide awake, thinking about the night's unusual turn of events.

After leaving Ashley at her door, he had returned to his apartment. He'd stripped off his clothes and grabbed a pair of sweatpants. He had just pulled them on when he heard his doorbell. He'd thought it could only be Ashley. Though the idea of having a woman friend to hang out with where he could just be himself was something new for him, he'd liked it. And he liked Ashley. The warm glow of the afternoon they'd spent together still clung to his senses as he'd gone to answer the door.

Julie hadn't waited to be asked in. She'd stepped past him, trailing her fingers across his bare chest as she'd kicked the door shut.

Several hours had now passed since he'd gotten rid of Julie. She had used every trick she knew to try to persuade him to partake of what she freely offered. He had finally managed to tactfully direct her out of his apartment without being too rude, but it was obvious that she was not accustomed to being turned down.

He continued to toss and turn, then finally climbed out of bed. He wandered aimlessly around his living room, finally ending up in the kitchen where he fixed himself a scotch and water.

The rain had stopped. He took his glass out to the balcony, his bare feet and bare chest exposed to the cold damp air. A slight shiver went up his spine as a chill spread through his body, but he continued to stand on the balcony sipping from his glass and staring out into the darkness. His earlier encounter with Julie still upset him. As recently as six months ago he probably would not have turned her down, but that was then. Now things were different. It might seem to the casual observer that he had it all, but the truth was not that easy. His life was in shambles, and he didn't know what to do about it. Just when he thought he had rid himself of the past, memories from four years ago forced their way into his consciousness.

He was to be married, the wedding only one week

away. The arrangements had been finalized. He phoned Joan as he did every morning when he woke. Only on that particular morning he got the telephone company recording saying the service had been disconnected. He had driven to her apartment, concerned that something was wrong, and had been informed by the landlord that she'd moved out the night before with no forwarding address. Two days later he received a letter from her, saying she had run off to Las Vegas to marry a former boyfriend.

The experience had produced an odd mixture of emotions. There was the obvious hurt and anger mixed with feelings of betrayal. But there had also been a curious sense of relief that confused him at the time. After months of agonizing, he finally admitted to himself that he had been having very serious doubts as to whether he really loved her as much as he thought he did or was simply caught up in the emotional whirlwind. It had been Joan—not him—who had pushed for them to get married.

The actual incident had long since ceased to be of importance, but the emotional scars ran deep. He dated lots of different women, but had refused to invest his emotions. He refused to become involved in a relationship and, in fact, actually ran at the first hint of commitment. Sex without any emotional attachment had been the norm for the past four years. He'd vowed never to allow himself to be vulnerable again.

Lately he had grown tired of the routine, of the shallowness and emptiness of his existence. He had his work. He loved flying, but he wanted more out of life. His fears continued to outweigh his desires. He could not bring himself to expose that vulnerable side he had been carefully protecting for the past few years. He had been living by a credo that said if he did not invest his emotions, then he could not be hurt. But there was a fear that ran even deeper in him than his dread of commitment. It was the possibility he had closed himself off so completely that even if the right woman did come along he would not recognize her. He questioned whether he was even capable of falling in love.

The sound of a sliding door coming from the next apartment interrupted his reflections. He walked over to the side railing when Ashley appeared on her balcony wearing a long warm robe and heavy wool socks. "Hi. You're up late. Couldn't you sleep, either?"

The sound of a man's voice coming out of the darkness startled her. She gasped as she felt her heart leap into her throat. But as soon as she saw Britt she relaxed. She placed her hand on her chest and breathed a sigh of relief as she spoke. "You scared the life out of me. You should feel my heart pounding."

"Should I? Give me a second, I'll be right over."

He caught her totally off guard by his impulsive action. She watched as he hopped up on the side railing of his balcony and jumped across to her balcony, carefully guarding what was left of his drink. He wiggled his fingers in front of her face, a slight grin tugging at the corners of his mouth.

"Now what am I supposed to be feeling and where is it?" He took a step back, his impish look changing to one of feigned caution as his silvery eyes twinkled in the dim light. "Wait a minute. This doesn't have anything to do with that veracity of yours, does it?"

"You're impossible," was all she could get out between fits of laughter that she could not contain.

"I may not be easy, but I'm far from impossible. I can most definitely be had. Wanna try me?" He shot her his best comical leer as he arched an eyebrow and cocked his head.

He looked into her eyes, and an instant later a realization flashed through him like a bolt of lightning. She was too comfortable to be with and that was a very dangerous thing. She was not at all like the string of fast women he had been associating with over the past four years. She was the type a man could really fall hard for. He tentatively lifted his hand to her face, his fingers lightly tracing the outline of her upper lip.

Ashley felt something she did not want to feel—a strong attraction to this very disconcerting man. She could not allow herself to become involved with another blatant womanizer. The unpleasant memories of her engagement to Jerry Broderick still grated against a tender spot inside her.

The feel of Britt's fingers against her skin made her shiver, a quivering sensation that started deep inside and spread to the surface. She knew in an instant that this was a very dangerous man. He was too charming, too sexy—too desirable. He was just the type of man that a woman could really fall hard for. He was also the type of scoundrel who would most definitely break a woman's heart. She had been there before and had sworn she would not let it happen again.

She stepped back from his all-too-tempting touch, took a steadying breath and quickly changed the subject. "You're going to catch pneumonia standing out here in this cold, damp air with hardly anything on, especially with your bare feet." She placed her foot on top of his, her heavy wool sock scraping softly against his skin. "And if you're sick, who's going to take me sight-seeing in the morning?"

"I'll tell you what. If I'm sick in bed, you can sit by my side and nurse me back to health." He shot her an appraising look. "How are your nursing skills? I'll tell you right now, I'm a terrible patient. I'm very demanding and require around-the-clock care and lots of very *personal* attention.'' He lowered his voice in a seductive manner and leaned close to her. His words tickled across her ear in a sexy whisper. ''I'm particularly fond of sponge baths.''

She felt the crimson heat rise on her cheeks. She refused to give in to his too smooth and highly perfected line. She returned his same teasing manner. ''You're a terrible patient? Well, buster, my nursing skills are abysmal so you'd just better stay healthy!''

He stared at her in mock disbelief. ''*Buster?* That's pretty tough talk.''

She lightly tapped his chest with her index finger. ''And don't you forget it, either.'' Her words were emphatic, but the twinkle in her eyes belied any animosity.

He quickly captured her hand in his and held it against his bare chest. Her hand felt warm and soft, her touch inviting. He looked at her for a long serious moment, then released her hand and grinned. ''I never forget a thing, especially when it sounds life threatening.''

She was thankful he had released her hand. His touch conveyed warmth, and the feel of his hard chest sent a tingle of excitement through her fingertips. She returned his grin. ''I'm glad that's finally settled.''

There was a long moment of silence between them. He took the last swallow of his scotch then looked at the glass in his hand. ''I'm down to only ice cubes. I guess I should take that as a sign to call it a night.'' His expression brightened as he spoke with new enthusiasm. ''I've got an idea. Why don't you come over to my place for breakfast in the morning? I whip up a mean omelet.''

''That sounds great. I haven't had a chance to do any

serious grocery shopping yet, so my refrigerator is a little bare. What time?''

"I'm usually an early riser. Is seven o'clock okay? We could make it later if that's too early for you.''

"I'm an early riser, too. That'll be perfect. Are we still going sight-seeing after breakfast?''

"Just try and stop us.'' He leaned forward and placed a kiss on her forehead then jumped back to his own balcony. "Good night, Ashley. I'll see you later.''

She watched as he went back inside his apartment and closed the balcony door. She continued to watch as the light coming from inside his apartment dimmed when he closed the drapes, plunging the balcony into complete darkness.

Ashley went to bed, but remained awake for a while, lost in thought. Finally she turned off the light and closed her eyes.

Once again the image of Britt's well-defined physique played across her mind.

Britt leaned forward in bed, his head between his hands and a box of tissues by his side. A glass of water and a bottle of aspirin sat on the nightstand. He grabbed for the tissue box as another sneeze started to build. The raspiness in his throat hurt when he tried to swallow.

He glanced at the clock—six-thirty in the morning. Reluctantly he hauled himself out of bed and trudged listlessly toward his bathroom. A slight shiver ran through his body as he turned on the hot water.

He made a game attempt at getting dressed, following his shower. He wore a new pair of gray Dockers, a bright red crew neck sweater and even managed to pull on a pair of matching red socks. He wandered into the kitchen and immediately became aware of the absence of the aroma of freshly brewed coffee. A twinge of irritation pricked at him. He had forgotten to set the automatic timer.

He switched on the coffeepot, then poured himself a glass of orange juice and downed it in one long swig. The acidity of the citrus juice burned his raw throat. He'd started to gather the ingredients he needed for the omelette—eggs, milk, mushrooms, green onions and bell peppers—when the doorbell rang.

He caught just a hint of Ashley's perfume, a light fragrance with spicy undertones that tickled his senses, when she entered the apartment. He helped her out of her jacket, then showed her into the living room. His gaze never left her as she walked across the room to his couch. He mustered the best grin he could, considering his head was spinning and his entire body ached from head to toe. ''Forget the omelette, you look good enough to be breakfast. Are you always this enticing so early in the morning?''

His words triggered her annoyance. Did he ever give it a rest? She started to snap out an answer, but stopped when she got a good look at him. ''Are you all right?'' She noticed the dull glassiness that had replaced the sparkle in his eyes; his skin looked flushed and he unconsciously scratched at his throat. She placed her hand on his forehead. ''You're burning up.''

He quickly pulled her hand away, even though her touch felt cool and soothing. ''I'm fine, really. Just a mild touch of the flu coming on. You were right, I shouldn't have been outside last night with my bare feet. I'll be okay, don't worry.'' He started to turn toward the kitchen. ''Coffee should be ready by now.''

She grabbed his arm, her concern clearly evident in her voice. ''You can forget about cooking anything. You're going right to bed. Now, which door is your bedroom?''

He made a valiant attempt at a lustful leer. "This is so sudden, Miss Thornton. I hardly know you. Besides, what makes you think I'm that type of man? Perhaps I'm saving myself for…" His voice faded off into a raspy croak. He pointed toward his bedroom door and let her take charge. His head was really spinning now, and the air felt like the inside of a refrigerator.

He collapsed on his back across the king-size bed, his long legs dangling over the end. His face was very flushed and his forehead wet with perspiration. He started to shiver.

"Come on, Britt, you've got to get under the covers where you'll be warm." She bent over and put her arms around him, trying to raise him up into a sitting position.

He reached out and pulled her down on top of him. His raspy voice was barely audible, but he managed a feeble smile. "Will you get under here with me? Your body heat pressed against mine will be twice as warm."

She struggled out of his arms and looked at him as she shook her head, her irritation combined with just a hint of amusement. "Don't you ever give it a rest?" She felt his feverish brow and noted his glazed eyes. "Here you are with what has to be a high temperature, and you're trying to make a pass at me." She muttered the words more to herself than to him, even though she did say them out loud. "I have a feeling you'll still be making passes from the grave."

An attempt at a laugh escaped his lips. "You're probably right." He grimaced as he tried to get up, then fell back on the bed. "Help me get out of these clothes, will you?"

She eyed him suspiciously, but quickly realized his words were not the result of an overactive libido. She helped him to sit up, then pulled his sweater over his head.

He fell back on the bed with his eyes closed. She paused, uncertain how to proceed. Finally she bent over and unsnapped his pants. Her fingers trembled as she lifted the tab on the zipper. She hesitated a moment before lowering it. She refused to admit that it was embarrassment or anxiety causing her heart to pound—it was a curious sort of anticipation.

She stood at the foot of the bed, grabbed the legs of his pants and began to pull. "You're going to have to give me a little help here. Can you at least raise your rear end off the bed?" He arched his hips upward as she yanked on the pants legs, then sank back into the bed as she finished removing them. A thin sheen of perspiration covered his face and chest. His breathing became labored and shallow.

She smiled inwardly, barely managing to suppress the grin that tugged at the corners of her mouth. His briefs were as bright as his sweater. She also noticed what great legs he had—long and muscular. She stared intently, her gaze traveling slowly up his shins then his thighs.

A raspy voice broke into her visual dalliance. "Could I interrupt your inspection tour?"

Her attention flew immediately to his lopsided little grin. She knew her face had to be as red as his briefs. It even felt red. She averted her eyes, too embarrassed to look at him.

"Could you get me the throat lozenges from the nightstand?" She pulled open the top drawer. "No, the second drawer!" he quickly shouted as best he could, considering his raw throat, but his words came too late.

She saw the assortment of condom packets. A few packets would certainly be understandable. But a selection of every type imaginable? It confirmed her already entrenched opinion of his overactive libido. He was just one more man who devoted his life to conquest and quantity, the type who could not be faithful to only one woman. Then she reminded herself of the nature of their relationship, one of friends who had separate lives and life-styles. She admitted to herself that her censure was inappropriate.

Britt groaned and pulled the covers up over his head. In what seemed like only seconds the rhythm of his breathing told her he had dozed off. She pulled the covers back and tucked them around his shoulders. His forehead still felt very hot. Sleep would probably be the best thing for him. She left the bedroom and wandered to the kitchen.

A little bit of guilt began to gnaw at her. Finding the packets in a drawer next to his bed should not have been a surprise. After all, he was a very attractive, sexy man. She heard the unwarranted contempt in her inner tone of voice. Once again she had allowed her personal experience to color her assessment of something that was clearly none of her business.

She struggled with the dilemma. Why was she so bothered by his personal life? The condoms were not sitting around in the open as if he were flaunting them. There was no doubt in her mind that he was a first-class womanizer, yet there was something very appealing about his open, easy manner—something very comfortable in spite of her misgivings about his character. She refused to take the thoughts any further, or perhaps she was reluctant to delve any deeper for fear that she might discover just how attractive she found him.

After helping herself to a cup of coffee, she wandered into the living room and sat on the couch, then surveyed the surroundings. His apartment was sparsely furnished and had little in the way of personal touches or accessories. The furniture—what there was of it—was in good taste and of good quality. It occurred to her that his bedroom was furnished in the same austere manner.

Her curiosity about the other room finally got the better of her good manners. After glancing back toward his bedroom, she went to the closed door, opened it and peeked in. It was a guest room that contained only a bed, dresser, one nightstand and lamp.

"Britt? Are you here?"

The sudden intrusion of a woman's voice startled her. She hurried to the living room to see what was going on and found a woman standing in the entry hall, the *same* woman she had seen with Britt before—Julie, he'd said her name was.

Julie's face registered her surprise at seeing a woman in Britt's apartment. Her breathy way of speaking disappeared and her voice took on a hard edge. "Just who are you? Where's Britt? Is he in here?" She started toward the closed bedroom door, and Ashley charged across the room to head her off.

Ashley caught up to her just as Julie opened the bedroom door. Ashley lowered her voice to a whisper. "He's sleeping. Please don't wake him. He has the flu and he's running a high temperature."

Julie brushed Ashley aside and rushed past her, putting her arms around Britt as she perched on the edge of his bed. "My poor darling. Is there anything I can do for you?"

Britt opened his eyes and tried to focus on Julie, finally managing a few words in a barely audible rasp. "Sorry, darlin', I can't come out and play. I'm confined to bed...alone."

Ashley's gaze moved curiously from Britt to Julie. As she contemplated the full meaning of his words, her glance snapped back to Britt. She leaned over to Julie and whispered, "Let him sleep," then waited for the woman to follow her from the room.

When the two women reached the living room, Julie took a moment to carefully scrutinize Ashley. Finally she spoke, her voice contemptuous. "I don't know who you are, but you'd better keep your hands off him. He's mine."

"Britt and I are neighbors." Then she added as an afterthought, "Just friends—nothing more." As she realized that she was *explaining* herself to this stranger, Ashley felt her anger build. Just who did this woman think she was? She had as much as accused Ashley of sleeping with Britt. Even if she did engage in casual sex, it would not be with someone like Britt Carlton. It would not be with a man who would surely end up breaking her heart.

Julie thrust out her overly developed chest and smirked while blatantly staring at Ashley's considerably less endowed figure. "I'm not worried. You don't have what it takes to satisfy a man like Britt Carlton." With that, she turned and walked out the front door, slamming it behind her.

Ashley's anger boiled as she glared at the space Julie had just vacated. She rotated her hips in an exaggerated manner, mimicking Julie's gestures. The words danced on the tip of her tongue, but she managed to keep them inside her head. *I'll tell you where you can put those oversize melons of yours—and I bet you'll have lots of room left over, too!*

Julie's words had produced an odd combination of anger and regret—anger at the accusation that she did not measure up to Britt's needs and regret that it was probably the truth. It would take a very special woman to capture Britt Carlton's heart and devotion.

Her anger returned full force—anger at herself for allowing Julie's words to matter. After all, Britt was not her type of man. And he definitely was *not* what she needed.

"Damn," she said to no one, her frustration finally escaping into the open.

3

A raspy laugh broke into Ashley's anger. She whirled around to find Britt standing about five feet from her.

She had been so preoccupied with her own thoughts that she had not heard him enter the room. Her mouth fell open and she felt her face flush a hot crimson. Finally she stammered, "I'm...I must apologize. I didn't realize you were there." She lowered her gaze to the floor, too embarrassed to make eye contact with him.

He placed his fingers under her chin and raised her face until he could see her eyes. In a voice that projected all the pain of his raw throat he whispered, "I'm the one who should be apologizing to you. You are my guest. You shouldn't have to defend yourself against uninvited troublemakers."

Suddenly his body convulsed with violent tremors and beads of sweat broke out across his forehead. She took his arm and turned him toward the bedroom. "It's back to bed for you—and yes...alone." He offered no resistance and made no glib remarks as she helped him across the room.

Once she'd settled him in bed, she tucked in the covers along the edge of his body and glanced at the clock. Nine-thirty. She had been at Britt's apartment for only two and a half hours. It had all the makings of a very long day.

She placed the throat lozenges on top of the nightstand next to the glass of water, aspirin bottle and box of tissues. "Do you want me to call your doctor? Maybe some antibiotics—"

"No, I'll be fine." He reached out and squeezed her hand. "Honest." He closed his eyes. "Ashley...I'm sorry about today's sight-seeing. I'll make it up to you." Then he drifted into a restless sleep.

For what seemed like several hours—but in reality was only two—she sat at the foot of the bed and watched him as he slept. He tossed and turned in a fitful manner, expressions of pain and anguish occasionally crossing his face. She knew a fever could cause the mind to conjure up strange thoughts and visions. She wondered what was going on in his head, what demons he battled in his subconscious. He mumbled incoherent words from time to time. She thought she could make out a name. At first she thought it sounded like Julie, but then she decided it was Joan.

He groaned as he kicked off the covers. His whole body glistened with perspiration. Then he became very still. The emotional turmoil disappeared from his face, his breathing slowed and he seemed much calmer. She heard him call her name as she pulled the covers up to his shoulders. "I'm here." He did not respond.

She studied his features. Why did the intelligent, funny, charming, handsome ones usually turn out to be scoundrels? She quickly shoved the negative thoughts away as new ones filled her mind—thoughts that brought a warm smile to her lips. Britt had made it very clear that she was a guest in his home and that Julie was not welcome. He had chosen her friendship over Julie's obvious sexual favors. Exactly what kind of man was he and what did he really want out of life? He was beginning to become a bit of a puzzle. Perhaps he was not as easily categorized as she'd thought and possibly more complex than she'd given him credit for.

She dampened a washcloth with cool water and placed it on his forehead. He furrowed his brow, then slowly opened his eyes and looked around as if trying to understand what was happening. He seemed disoriented. Bewilderment covered his face. He attempted to sit up, but she pushed him back down against the pillow. When he started to speak, she put her fingers to his lips.

"Don't talk, just nod your head. Do you have a thermometer?" He nodded and pointed toward the bathroom. "Your head feels very hot. If your temperature is even a tenth of a degree above 103, I'm going to call the paramedics." She saw the objection form on his face as he tried to get up.

She held him down, looked him squarely in the eyes and used her most stern and authoritative voice. "Don't you even dare think of trying to argue with me." With that, she went to the bathroom, retrieved the thermometer and stuck it in his mouth.

"Well, you just made it—102.8 degrees." She reached for the glass on the nightstand. "Here, you need to drink some water. You've lost a lot of fluids. You don't want to get dehydrated." Her hand cupped the back of his head, raising him a little as she held the glass to his lips. His wet hair clung to the back of his neck. It obviously pained him to swallow. She adjusted the covers around his shoulders as he closed his eyes and drifted off to sleep again.

So many questions. Why did he have this nice apartment, buy tasteful furniture, then leave his surroundings devoid of all personal touches and warmth? Not even a single photograph of his family. It was almost as if he considered the apartment a place to eat and sleep but not really his home. And who was Joan? And where did Julie fit into his life?

She had categorized Britt as a wanton womanizer, the only problem being that his surroundings did not fit the image. His was the stereotypical bachelor pad usually associated with the swinging singles life-style, yet it was somehow different. It almost seemed to reflect a life-style devoid of anything personal and warm—sanitized so that it was free of anything revealing about the occupant. She wondered who was the real Britt Carlton. She gave a brief thought to the packets of condoms, but again dismissed it as being none of her business.

That was not the type of relationship she had with Britt. They were friends. Even though they had only known each other three days, she felt confident in making that statement. It was strange the way it had all happened so quickly. One minute he was standing at her front door yelling at her about making noise and the next minute they were joking and teasing as if they had been friends for years. It was a comfortable rapport without pressure. It felt right.

He moaned and turned onto his side, drawing her attention. She put her hand on his forehead. He still felt hot. She dampened the washcloth and wiped his face and brow again. His hair was wet with perspiration. She brushed it back from his face with her fingers. Her hand lingered, as if it had a will of its own. Her fingers traced his lips and then his jawline. Even flushed and sweaty, he was very handsome.

Just then he opened his eyes and reached his hand out from under the covers. He touched her cheek and tried to smile. She took his hand and put it back under the covers. "I'll get you some water."

She returned with the refilled water glass, raised his

head and put the glass to his lips. As he drank, she noticed his eyes were not as glazed as they had been, but they still reflected his feverish condition.

Once he was sleeping soundly, she returned to the living room. He probably would not be needing her any longer, but she did not want to leave him alone quite yet. She reached for the phone and dialed her parents in Wichita, charging the call to her phone.

Ashley talked for almost half an hour, filling her family in on her new apartment and telling them about Britt. After she hung up, she again checked on him. He was still sleeping. Suddenly the ringing phone intruded into the quiet.

"Hello." There was only silence on the other end. "Hello? Is anyone there?"

A woman's voice finally spoke. "Is this Britt Carlton's number?"

"Yes, it is. He's in bed with the flu. I'm his neighbor. May I take a message?"

The female voice on the other end became friendlier. "Oh, you must be Darlene from upstairs. We've never met. My name is Cindy. I haven't heard from Britt for a while and was just wondering why. But I don't want to bother him if he's sick. Just tell him Cindy called and said she really *needs* him."

"Sure thing, Cindy."

"Bye, now." Cindy hung up, leaving Ashley staring at the receiver in her hand.

"Who was that?"

She jumped as Britt's raspy voice startled her out of her thoughts. She turned and saw him leaning against the door frame of his bedroom. "What are you doing out of bed?"

"The phone woke me."

"That was someone named Cindy who said to tell you—" she paused as she tried to hide a combination of annoyance and amusement at what she assumed was just one of many female callers "—that she *needs* you. I don't want to say she sounded overly anxious, but I think it's probably a good thing that I locked your front door after Julie left, otherwise you might have had another visitor."

He groaned and looked up at the ceiling. "I'm a sick man. Give me a break. Show me a little mercy."

"I've been showing you mercy all day," she said, then felt his forehead. She couldn't tell if it felt any cooler, but it didn't seem to be any hotter. "How do you feel?"

"I feel like hell."

"You'd better get back in bed or else put on some clothes before you start shivering again." She had expected some type of remark from him, some comment. Instead, he silently turned and went back to his bed, climbed under the covers and closed his eyes. She followed him and seated herself on the edge of his bed.

"Here, put this under your tongue." A couple of minutes later she removed the thermometer. "It still says 102.8 degrees." She placed the damp washcloth against his forehead, then tucked the blankets tightly around his shoulders when he began shivering again. "I want to call your doctor. I'm sure he'll be able to prescribe something. What's his name and phone number?"

"I told you, I'll be okay."

"I know what you told me and I know what I'm seeing." She wanted him to know by her take-no-prisoners attitude that she did not intend to take any flack from him. "Now, how do I find your doctor?"

He gave up trying to dissuade her. "Call Ellen at my office. She'll get in touch with our flight doctor. The number's in the front of my address book next to the phone."

She glanced at the clock. It was only two in the afternoon even though it seemed much later. She went in search of the address book and returned a few minutes later. "I talked to Ellen and she's calling your doctor. She says she'll have something delivered from the pharmacy right away."

He moaned softly. She did not know if it was in response to what she had said or simply a sign of his discomfort while he slept. She wandered toward a bookcase in the corner of his bedroom. She studied the books. His reading tastes seemed to cover a wide variety of interests, both fiction and nonfiction. She picked up one of the books and carried it over to the bed. She sat on the corner and started skimming through the book.

Another two hours passed before he began to stir again. His tremors increased. He turned on his side and curled his body into a ball, instinctively trying to use his own body heat to keep himself warm. She glanced at her watch, wondering when the pharmacy would deliver the medicine. He reached out from under the blankets and grabbed her arm, tugging her down toward him. "I'm c-c-cold. I'm v-v-very c-cold." He pulled her under the blankets and buried his face in her neck while wrapping his arms tightly around her. His trembling hands found their way under her blouse. She tried to unwrap his arms from around her, but he shivered in hard spasms as he held her tighter, his hands moving erratically across her bare midriff.

She gasped as she felt his fingers brush lightly across her nipple and back again, then his entire hand closed over her bare breast and remained there. She gulped then swallowed hard in an attempt to maintain her calm.

His sensual touch sent tremors through her body, but they were far different from his flu-induced shivering. Her tremors ignited a glow of excitement that she neither wanted nor welcomed. She felt his warm breath tickle across her ear, then his words penetrated the erotic fog that had clouded her mind and prevented her from immediately untangling their bodies.

"Lovely lady...could I talk you into running away with me for a weekend of fun and games? Just you and me and a water bed..."

She closed her eyes as the vivid image formed in her mind, then took a calming breath. This had to stop and it had to stop right now. She firmly grasped his hand, pulled it away from her breast, unwrapped his other arm from around her waist, then slid toward the edge of the bed and out from under the covers.

Britt reached his hand out to her. "Don't g-g-go away."

The doorbell rang. She leaned over and spoke to him, her voice not as calm and controlled as she would have liked as the unexpected excitement of his touch heated her senses. "Someone is at the door. I'll be right back."

Moments later, as she returned to his bedroom, she said, "Your medication has arrived," then read the instructions on the label of the prescription bottle. She took two tablets from the bottle and picked up the glass of water. "Here, take these."

She watched as he swallowed the medication. Her logic told her that he had no knowledge of what he had said or done, but it didn't change the way the tremors of excitement insisted on lingering. It also did not prevent her from wondering exactly what a fantasy weekend with Britt Carlton would be like.

Five hours had passed since Britt had taken the medication. His violent shivering had stopped, his forehead did not feel as hot, and he was sleeping peacefully. It had been a long and very tiring day. All she wanted was to go to bed and get some much-needed sleep, but she still felt uneasy about leaving him alone. She sighed and headed for the guest bedroom. Without even bothering to take off her clothes, she flopped across the bed and fell into an exhausted sleep.

She had no idea how long she had been sleeping when a sharp noise woke her. She rushed toward the sound, shaking the sleep from her mind. As she entered Britt's bedroom, she spotted him coming out of his bathroom. She placed her hand on his forehead. His head did not feel as hot. His gray eyes were dull and watery, his hair a tousled mess, his cheeks and chin covered with whisker stubble—and he still wore only his red briefs. He did not seem as disoriented as earlier, and he had stopped shivering.

"Are you okay? Do you need anything?"

"Ashley…" He seemed surprised to see her. He furrowed his brow and stared at her for a moment as if trying to collect his thoughts. "What time is it?" he asked, his voice still raw. "Or maybe I should ask what day it is."

"You haven't been out of it that long." She glanced at the clock on his nightstand. "It's three o'clock in the morning, so you've been in bed about twenty hours." She felt his forehead again then picked up the thermometer. "Here, put this under your tongue. I think your fever is coming down."

He put the thermometer in his mouth and climbed back in bed, then pulled the blankets up across his chest before reaching out to grab her hand. He gave it a weak squeeze, indicating how much of his strength and energy had been drained from his body. She removed the thermometer from his mouth.

"Well, it's down to 101.6. That's very encouraging."

"Marked down from what? It must not have gone over 103 since you didn't have the paramedics cart me off to some unknown place."

She grinned at him. "So you *do* know what's been happening. Marked down from 102.8 degrees."

His expression turned serious as he scrunched his mouth to one side and furrowed his brow in concentration. "Actually, I don't remember much of anything after you went to call Ellen."

She studied him for a long moment. Her thoughts darted back to the sensation of his fingers brushing her nipple and his warm hand closing over her breast, to the tremor of excitement caused by his touch. She shook away the tantalizing memory. "You seemed to be very cold, you were shivering so violently. After the prescription arrived and you took the medication, you settled down and went to sleep."

"Have you been here the whole time?"

"I was afraid to leave you alone, and I certainly wasn't going to leave you in Julie's care."

He wrinkled his nose and cocked his head, then the light of recognition came to his face. "Oh, yeah. I remember now." He frowned as he continued to speak in a raspy voice. "I'm sorry I wasn't there to intervene. I heard what she said to you, but by the time I was able to drag myself out of bed and get to the living room she was stomping out the door. You handled the situation in a very classy manner—right up until your little dance after she left."

He smiled at her, a lopsided impish little grin. "That wasn't classy—that was totally outrageous. I loved it." He squeezed her hand again. "You're definitely no milquetoast. Remind me to stay on your good side."

"You can stay on my good side if you promise not to put me through this nurse stuff again. If this is your idea of showing a lady a good time, then I beg to be excused in the future." Her attempt at an authoritarian expression failed miserably when she could not control the little grin that turned the corners of her mouth.

He looked into her eyes, his gaze embracing her. "Ashley, in case I didn't apologize to you earlier about that Julie business, I want to—"

"Don't worry about it. You did apologize and the whole thing's forgotten."

"All right then, how about this? I know I haven't told you how much I appreciate your looking after me. This is really unusual. I haven't had the flu—or whatever this is—in five years. I'm really very healthy…honest."

"Oh, sure. That's easy for you to say." She picked up the prescription bottle and removed two tablets, then handed them to him along with a glass of water. "Here, you're overdue for your medication."

He swallowed the tablets. "You women are all alike, aren't you? You take away a guy's pants, get him in bed so that he's totally helpless and completely in your power, then you inflict unspeakable punishment on him."

She made an unsuccessful attempt to project a harsh scowl. "Yes…I can see you're definitely feeling better. If you don't behave yourself, I'm going to be forced to tell you what really happened here." She leaned over the bed and pulled the covers around his shoulders.

He looked up at the ceiling and groaned. "I don't think I want to know." His gaze settled on her for a moment before he asked sheepishly, "Did I do anything I shouldn't have? I didn't embarrass myself, did I? Or embarrass you?" he added hesitantly, almost shyly, as if he were not sure he really wanted to hear the answer.

Her mind went to the sensation of his fingers on her bare skin, brushing her nipple, his hand caressing her breast. Her gaze focused on his mouth. It made her even more curious about what type of lover he would be. She shook her head slightly to rid it of the uninvited and totally unacceptable thought that had popped into her mind.

She smiled warmly in an attempt to put him at ease about his obvious concerns. "No, you didn't do anything wrong. Now go back to sleep."

As she made her retreat, he asked quietly, "Would you stay the rest of the night?"

She returned to his side. "Sure, there's no point in my going home now. I'll be in the other bedroom if you need anything." She put her hand on his forehead, then gently smoothed his hair back with her fingers.

"Thanks." As he drifted off to sleep his thoughts went to a hazy memory—the feel of silky smooth skin, a taut nipple, a perfectly shaped tantalizing form that exactly suited his hand. He finally sank into the soft darkness of a peaceful sleep.

Ashley was not as easily lulled to sleep. The vivid memory of his tingling caress disturbed her. Under no circumstances could she allow herself to feel anything toward Britt beyond simple friendship and concern for a fellow human being in need. However, her conscious thoughts did nothing to dampen the excitement that sizzled inside her as she closed her eyes and recalled the sensation of his touch. She finally dropped into a fitful sleep.

A clattering sound woke Ashley. She looked around the room and tried to get her bearings. She was in Britt's guest room and it was daylight outside. Slowly she sat up and ran her fingers through her mussed hair then slid out of bed and made her way to the living room.

"Good morning, Sleepyhead." The raspy voice that came from the kitchen called a cheery greeting. "I was beginning to think you were going to sleep the entire day."

His gaze drifted over her appearance as she walked into the kitchen. "You look like you've been through a rough day...and a rough night." Flashing her an impish grin, he continued, "What in the world have you been up to?"

Britt filled the pot with the proper amount of water and poured it into the coffeemaker. He was dressed in old jeans and a T-shirt with his hair still damp from the shower.

"Well, you seem to be in a better mood."

"Why shouldn't I be in a good mood? It's a beautiful day. The sun is shining and the birds are singing."

She carefully scrutinized his appearance and noted his easy smile. "I take it that you're feeling much better then."

He continued in an upbeat manner. "Absolutely. You pumped me full of antibiotics and I had a good night's sleep."

"I'm glad one of us feels rested." Her voice carried a hint of annoyance.

He arched one eyebrow as he looked at her with all the innocence he could muster. "What's the matter? Didn't you have a good night's sleep?"

She glared at him without answering.

"Hmm...you're obviously not a morning person. Well, maybe I can tempt you with some breakfast...or should I say, brunch?"

"Brunch? What happened to breakfast?"

"Well, the day is half gone," he said as though the answer was obvious.

She looked around for a clock. "What time is it?"

"It's now ten-fifteen."

"Ten-fifteen? Oh, no. I can't believe I slept this late." She looked down at her clothes. "I'm a mess. I'll run home and get cleaned up while you prepare that breakfast you still owe me. I want to take a quick shower. I should be back in about half an hour."

"A shower? You can take a shower here." A grin played across his lips as he lowered his raspy voice almost to a whisper. "I'd feel honored if you'd allow me to scrub your back." He leaned over and whispered in her ear. "I won't peek...honest. I'll keep my eyes closed the entire time." He teasingly blew in her ear.

Her nostrils flared as she breathed in his clean masculine scent mixed with his aftershave. "It won't do you any good to blow in my ear. I'm immune to that type of blatant come-on."

She put her hand against his chest and pushed him away from her until he was at arm's length, what she hoped would be a safe distance. She studied him while trying to decide how to handle the situation. She shook her head in resignation as she tried to suppress the grin that tugged at the corners of her mouth. "Yep...no doubt about it. You're definitely feeling much better. I'll see you in a little while."

He watched as she grabbed her purse and jacket, then headed out his front door. A hazy memory of a soft body with delectable curves tried to crystallize in his mind. The memory was almost there, but he could not fully retrieve it.

He went to his bathroom, picked up the prescription bottle and read the instructions. He took two more tablets and downed them with a glass of water, then looked at his reflection in the mirror. He did not know which was worse, the way he looked or the way he felt. He had made an effort to act fine in front of Ashley, but the truth of the matter was that he still felt lousy.

He went to his bedroom and picked up his clothes from the day before. He put the Dockers and sweater in the basket for the dry cleaners and tossed his briefs and socks in the hamper. Finally he yanked the blankets from the bed. As he pulled off the top sheet, he caught the faintest whiff of the perfume Ashley had worn when she first arrived at his apartment. He gathered up the bottom sheet. Again, the same fragrance lingered, only a little bit stronger. A troubled thought crossed his mind as he removed the feather pillows from the pillow cases. One of the cases also held the scent of her perfume.

How had the scent gotten there? It was a disturbing question, one that he was not sure he wanted an answer to. He shoved the disturbing thoughts from his mind and busied himself putting clean sheets on the bed. He refused to dwell on the possibilities.

As soon as Ashley entered her apartment she pulled off her clothes, threw them in the hamper and turned on the shower. She grabbed her brush and ran it through her hair while waiting for the water to heat up. Her mind went back to Britt—the remembered sensation of what had happened in his bed caused her nipples to pucker. She slammed down the hairbrush, disgusted with herself over her thoughts and her unexpected reaction to them.

She stepped into the warm spray of the shower, hoping it would wash away any errant sensual thoughts about Britt Carlton that might be lingering in her consciousness. She was determined to be just friends with him and not let it go beyond that. Still…there was something about him that truly excited her. A hint of sadness entered her thoughts. Was she doomed to always be attracted to the wrong type of man? First Jerry Broderick and now Britt Carlton? She wanted a home and family. Hopefully she would be able to find a caring man who would want the same thing she did—commitment in a solid relationship.

4

$\xrightarrow{\hspace{2cm}}\xleftarrow{\hspace{2cm}}$

Ashley swallowed the last bite of her omelette, then placed the fork on her empty plate. "You're right, Britt, you do whip up a mean omelet. That was delicious. You'll certainly make someone a good wife some day," she teased as she cocked her head and extended a mischievous grin. "Do you also know how to sew?"

"A wife?" He scrunched his face up and feigned a disagreeable expression. "That sounds ominously like marriage." He chuckled as if a thought had just occurred to him. "I've managed to survive thirty-one years without being trapped. There's no reason to change a winning streak."

Marriage... She had not meant for the conversation to take a turn down that road. "You still seem to really know your way around the kitchen, though, especially for—"

He turned to face her, fixing her with a questioning look. "Were you going to say, *especially for a man?*"

She averted her gaze as she felt the flush spread across her cheeks. "Yes, I'm afraid I was." She looked up in time to catch his quizzical expression. "You just don't seem like the type of man who would be doing anything more difficult than popping something into the microwave."

He eyed her with amusement. "Grab your coffee, and let's go into the living room."

She followed him into the other room and sat on the end of the couch while he sat cross-legged on the floor facing her. "Now, just what type of man do you think I am? Go ahead, be brutally honest." He flinched and put one hand in front of his face, as if deflecting a blow. "I can take it," he teased.

She saw no reason to spoil the light and easy mood with her truthful assessment of his character. So instead she laughed and said, "You're outrageous!"

"Whew! I'm glad that's over." His twinkling eyes turned serious as he reached out and ran his fingertips lightly across the back of her hand. "But that doesn't answer my question, does it?"

Britt searched the depths of her eyes. He wanted to know more about her, much more. She was so different from the women he had become accustomed to—women like Julie and Cindy. By contrast, Ashley was so real and honest, exactly what she appeared without any pretenses. She was like a breath of fresh air blowing away the storm clouds that had filled his life for the past four years.

She squirmed uncomfortably on the couch as she shifted her position, drawing one leg up under her. The conversation had taken a much-too-serious turn. She quickly changed the subject. "I was wondering, you have this nice apartment and nice furniture but there's not one personal touch here. It's almost as if you didn't really live here. Is there any reason why your apartment is so...so sterile?"

He shifted his weight, the movement awkward and seemingly ill at ease. "I don't know. I guess I just haven't gotten around to decorating since I moved in."

"Oh? Are you new to the building, too? How long have you lived here?"

His gaze seemed focused on a faraway place. A great sadness filled his eyes. He answered without any inflection in his voice. "I've lived here four years."

Britt furrowed his brow as he looked around, as if seeing his own apartment for the first time. "You know, you're right. I really need to do something with this place." He offered her an engaging smile. "That might be a good project for us to do later this week."

He quickly glanced at the floor in a surprisingly shy manner, then looked up into her eyes. "That was rather presumptuous of me. Let me try it again." He cleared his throat and squared his shoulders, instantly becoming all business as he spoke in a matter-of-fact tone of voice. "Would you mind giving me a hand decorating my apartment?" His familiar, practiced smile returned along with a teasing glint in his eyes. "I know, I know…I'm already so far in your debt now that I'll never get out."

She chuckled. "A little further in my debt and you could be my slave for life." The total impact of her spontaneous comment hit her a second later. She tried to hide her embarrassment over its implication by adopting a businesslike attitude. "I'd be happy to help you decorate your apartment."

He shot her a comical leer, refusing to let her initial choice of words drop. "Your slave for life? That sounds very interesting, but nothing too kinky—okay?"

"*Kinky* is in the eye of the beholder," she teased back. "You're just going to have to take your chances."

He scooted closer to her, obviously warming to the easy nature of their banter. "Does your eye behold *kinky* as having any connection with whipped cream, flavored oil or body paints?" Suddenly his smile faded and he furrowed his brow as if in deep concentration. He looked at her questioningly. "Wait a minute—you're not thinking in terms of things made out of leather, are you?"

She laughed with him, enjoying the surprising lightness of the moment. Being with him felt very comfortable—perhaps a bit too comfortable. She cleared her throat and glanced at her watch. "It's getting late. I'd better get home and take care of my own business." She rose from the couch and carried her coffee cup into the kitchen. "You, on the other hand, need your rest or you'll be back where you were yesterday."

He followed her to the kitchen, placed his hands on her shoulders and turned her around to face him. He looked searchingly into her eyes. "If we could be serious for a moment...I want to tell you how much I appreciate your staying with me yesterday, even the fact that you insisted on calling my doctor over my objections. What you did was more than I would have asked of a close friend or relative, let alone someone I've only known for a couple of days. I owe you a great deal, but I'm not sure what to do to repay you."

She held his eye contact, staring intently into the silvery depths. She felt the uneasiness stir in the pit of her stomach. She did not like the effect he had on her, an effect over which she seemed to have no control at all. "There's no reason for you to feel obligated to repay me, because there's nothing to repay." She forced what she hoped was an easy smile and casual manner. "Besides, I thought we were friends in spite of the fact that we've only known each other for a few days."

He maintained his serious approach. "You're not going to put me off that easily. I'll find something special that I can do to show my appreciation. I don't know what, but I'll find something." Having said what he wanted to say, he hushed her reply by gently placing his fingertips against her lips and kissing her forehead. "Case closed."

She emitted a sigh of resignation. "Okay…case closed. But for now, you make sure you take your medication and get some rest. I'll see you later."

Britt closed the front door after saying goodbye to Ashley. He wandered into his living room, then stretched out on the couch with his hands behind his head. Random thoughts darted through his mind, thoughts he was unable to put together into a neat and concise package. An uncomfortable feeling continued to poke at his consciousness, a nagging suspicion that Ashley had not told him everything that had happened during the hours that eluded his memory. If his suspicions were correct, then he hoped her decision to omit some details was not because of something he had done.

He shifted his gaze around the living room. It was the first time he had really taken the time to look at the furnishings and decor, to evaluate the message they projected. She was right. The room was devoid of all personality and warmth.

For the past four years he had been living an emotionally uninvolved life that had extended itself to his surroundings. But now—suddenly—he felt like doing something, felt like reaching out and embracing the world. He would start by adding a personal feel to his apartment. He smiled when he realized Ashley Thornton was the source of the light and warmth that had entered his life and caused his desire to make some changes. Yet an uneasy feeling tickled at the back of his mind, one he could not clearly place or interpret. It was almost as if he had made an unconscious decision to turn his apartment into a real home. When he combined that thought with his attraction to Ashley, it left him with a very disturbing realization, one he did not want to dwell on.

The next week flew by. Ashley and Britt had spent a great deal of time together, then he'd been gone for two days on a charter flight and she'd taken the opportunity to meet with Stuart Billington prior to starting her new job. She had also taken advantage of the time to get to know her other neighbors.

Two doors down, on the opposite side of the hallway, lived Shirley Whitcomb. Ashley had spent nearly two hours in Shirley's apartment and now knew far more about the woman than she thought possible for someone she had just met. She hadn't known what to think when Shirley shoved a key into her hand, telling her it was for the front door. The woman had gone on to explain that she was leaving on vacation in the morning and her brother would be stopping by to pick up the key.

Smiling at the memory, Ashley realized that Britt was due back tonight. She tried to force herself to relax, to quell the feeling of excitement that tried to work itself into her awareness as it grew closer to the hour he would be home.

The sudden sound of her doorbell sent a little thrill through her body. Her first thought was that Britt was home. But why was he ringing her doorbell? He'd taken to using her balcony door. She tightened the belt of her long robe and opened her door a crack. The young man standing on the other side was in his early twenties and neatly dressed. She did not recognize him.

"Ashley?"

"Yes..." She spoke cautiously, not sure what was going on. "Can I help you?"

"I'm Keith Whitcomb...Shirley's brother. She said I could pick up the key to her apartment from you."

Ashley relaxed and offered a smile as she opened the door so Keith could come in. "She said you'd be by sometime tonight." She went to the kitchen, retrieved the key from a drawer and handed it to him. "She said you were going to use her apartment for a few days. It's too bad your visit had to conflict with her business meetings in Los Angeles." They continued to talk for a couple of minutes, then she walked him to the front door. "If you need anything while you're here, give me a shout." She opened the door for him to leave.

"Thanks, I will. Good night."

As Keith turned to leave, Ashley looked up and saw Britt walking toward his apartment. The odd look on his face confused her. She gave him a friendly wave, which he returned, but he went to his own apartment instead of stopping. She closed her door. Perhaps he was just tired from his flight. She furrowed her brow and shook her head, still confused about what had just happened. His actions simply made no sense.

A quick flash of what could only be described as jealousy shot through Britt as he wondered exactly what had been going on. He did not like the looks of the man leaving Ashley's apartment or the fact that she was dressed in her robe and slippers. But even more than that, he was irritated with himself that it bothered him, which was the last thing he wanted to admit.

Maybe he should go over to her apartment and ask her who the man was and what he'd been doing there. No, that was a terrible idea that could only be interpreted as him prying into something that clearly was none of his business. Even though he had volunteered information about Julie and Cindy, she had not questioned him further about their significance in his life. He owed her the same courtesy of respecting her privacy. Besides, to ask would probably make him seem like a jealous fool.

To be jealous would mean he had a very personal interest in her that went way beyond being just friends, and he could not allow that to be so. He was not willing to put himself back into a situation where he could be hurt again—not now and not ever.

He liked Ashley very much, and he really enjoyed the time they spent together. It was such a relief to be able to be himself around a woman without any stress or pressure. But they could never be any more than just friends. That was the way it had to be. So why did he need to keep reminding himself?

The question still plagued him the next day when he and Ashley went shopping, but he made no mention of his concerns about what he had seen the previous night. And Ashley didn't bring it up, either, as she helped him pick out a few things for his apartment—wall hangings, pictures, houseplants and accessories.

Britt scrunched up his nose as he stared at the decorative pot Ashley held in her hand. "I don't know about all these plants—I mean, I like plants but they always die on me." He looked down at the floor then smiled sheepishly. "I always forget to water them." His expression suddenly brightened. "I know...I'll put you in charge of the plants. You insisted that I buy them, so you can be responsible for seeing that I water them."

They spent the rest of the afternoon in comfortable companionship, then spent the next few days sight-seeing. He took her on the Underground City tour in Pioneer Square, a harbor cruise on Elliott Bay, browsing in Pike's

Market, and watching the boats pass through the locks on the canal between Lake Washington and Puget Sound.

Each day brought them another step forward in solidifying a relationship that was gradually moving from a comfortable surface friendship to a deep and meaningful one. Yet neither of them felt confident enough to commit to the intimate type of relationship where the most deeply held secrets and fears were shared.

On one particularly clear and sunny afternoon they had lunch in the revolving restaurant at the top of the Space Needle.

"Oh, Britt. Look at this view. I can see forever—the Cascades, Mt. Rainier, the mountains on the Olympic Peninsula, all of Seattle at my feet. This is fantastic."

Her excitement was contagious. He studied her as she took in the sights. She seemed so open and genuinely enthralled with each new discovery. It was as if he were seeing things for the first time by looking at them through her eyes and sharing her joy.

"How would you like to check out the scenery from a little bit higher up?"

She looked at him quizzically, not fully understanding what he meant. "You mean from a taller building?" She scanned the skyline, trying to find a better vantage point.

"Not exactly." His mouth turned up at the corners as a mischievous grin took hold. He glanced at his watch. "Let me make a quick call, then we'll go." He headed for the pay phone.

She watched him as he walked away from the table, confidence radiating from each step of his smooth, sure stride. He was an emotionally dangerous man to be around—charming, intelligent, witty and far too sexy. Again, there was no doubt in her mind that he was a scoundrel who was incapable of making a commitment to one woman—exactly the type of man who was totally unacceptable.

One thing confused her, though—one thing that she could not reconcile with her assessment. They had spent so much time together that she was sure he could not possibly be seeing someone else. Even though his flirtatious behavior continued, he had made no overt moves toward her. The physical connection between them had been limited to casual pecks on the cheek or forehead, a quick brushing of the lips, his clasping her hand in his, putting his arm protectively around her shoulders—comfortable things, nothing more.

That was the way it should be. After all, they were just friends. So why did that one moment in his bed keep playing over and over in her mind? The moment when his hand closed over her breast? His whispered words about an illicit weekend of uninhibited lovemaking continued to pop into her consciousness at the most inopportune times. Why couldn't she make the thoughts go away? And why did they continue to excite her? Perhaps they were questions better left unanswered.

Britt returned from his phone call and they left the restaurant. A short while later he pulled his car up to the office of a charter company at the airport and escorted her inside the building. A woman in her fifties sat behind a desk in a large room, one entire wall covered with some sort of schedule board. "Ellen, this is Ashley Thornton. You two spoke on the phone during my recent... uh...illness."

The two women exchanged greetings, then he turned his attention to Ellen. "Is everything ready?" Receiving an affirmative nod, he grabbed Ashley's hand and led her out the door. Just outside, a small single-engine Cessna 210 sat on the tarmac.

Her eyes grew wide with surprise. "We're going up in an airplane?" An excited smile spread across her face.

"This is a perfect day for flying, clear and sunny. We'll be able to see for miles."

After a smooth takeoff, they flew over the city as Britt pointed out the sights, several of which they had recently visited by car and on foot. Then he headed the small plane north along Puget Sound. "We'll take a turn around the San Juan Islands before heading back to the airport."

She settled back in the seat, her excitement barely contained as each stunning new vista crossed her line of sight. They were well out over the water when he pointed toward an island on the far horizon. "That's the..."

His voice trailed off as his attention became riveted to the instrument panel. His features hardened into a tense expression as he tapped his finger on the glass, which covered one of the gauges. He quickly scanned the horizon.

A slight tremor of anxiety moved up her spine as she watched him. "Is something wrong?" He did not respond to her question, as if he had not heard her.

"Britt?"

His voice was calm and very much in control. "We have a little bit of a problem. The oil pressure gauge has dropped to nothing. My guess is that we've broken an oil line. We have maybe three minutes before the engine conks out." He reached for the radio and called in a distress signal identifying the plane, their position, their heading and his assessment of the problem.

Britt glanced over at her. "Don't be concerned. This baby can glide for quite a distance after the engine goes. We'll be perfectly okay." He reached over and gave her hand a quick squeeze and flashed her a confident smile.

She may have seemed in control on the outside, but

inside, her heart pounded like a bass drum and her pulse raced almost out of control. Her mouth felt dry, and she experienced a bit of difficulty swallowing. She did have enough of her wits about her to know that the last thing Britt needed at that moment was a frightened, hysterical passenger to deal with. "Is there something I should be doing, something that would help?" Her voice was not as firm as she would have liked.

He gave her hand another squeeze. "Don't worry. We'll be fine." He spoke rapidly, splitting his attention between flying the plane and instructing her. "We may have to ditch in the water. You'll find a floatation package and some life jackets under the seat behind you. See if you can get them out. Put one of the jackets on and give the other one to me."

She immediately turned her efforts to the task he had assigned her, even though her hands were shaking. After freeing the gear, she turned to him for more instructions. Her heart pounded so hard she feared it would actually burst from her chest.

He continued to scan the horizon. "If we do have to ditch in the water, make sure your door is ajar before we hit. This plane will glide, but it absolutely will not float. If your door is closed, the outside water pressure will prevent you from getting it open. As soon as we hit the water, get out of the plane as fast as you can."

She offered him a feeble smile and nodded that she understood his instructions.

Suddenly the engine sputtered then died. A suffocating silence totally engulfed them. She quickly looked at Britt. His face was set in an expressionless mask, his gaze constantly darting between the instrument panel and the surrounding area. He pointed straight ahead.

"There...I think we can make that."

She shaded her eyes with her hand as she peered into the bright sun. "Make what?"

"That island—there's a small landing strip on it. It's private, but this is an emergency." He glanced at her again, his face registering his concern. "I don't want to alarm you, but it's going to be close. If we luck out with some updrafts, we'll be okay. If not…" His voice trailed off and she understood. If not, then they would be ditching in the ocean. She took a deep breath, swallowed hard and waited for whatever was going to happen. Time seemed nearly suspended, the waiting almost too excruciatingly unbearable to handle.

"We're not going to make it, we're going in the water." His sharply clipped words reached out and grabbed her. "As soon as the plane stops, get out as quickly as you can. Don't wait for anything. Now get that door open and hang on. We're going in."

She felt the thud as the plane hit, felt the cold water splash into the cabin through the open door. She let out a gasp as the full impact of the situation engulfed her. In a matter of seconds the plane came to a stop and settled into the water. She unfastened her seat belt and jumped out the door immediately, as she had been instructed to do. The cold water closed around her, making her very grateful for the life jacket.

Britt grabbed the floatation kit, gave one last look to make sure she had gotten out safely, then went out his door just as the plane sank beneath the surface. He quickly pulled the release and inflated the raft, then reached for Ashley.

She swam toward him, the unfamiliar life jacket making her movements awkward. The water chilled her body. She tried to ignore it as she concentrated on reaching the raft. She felt his fingers wrap around her arm and pull her toward him. He helped her into the raft, then climbed in after her. He folded her into his arms. She tried to say something, but ended up coughing instead.

His voice showed his concern as much as his words. "Are you all right? You're not hurt, are you?"

"No, I'm fine." The seawater she had swallowed caused her to cough and gasp, but she knew she was all right. "Wet and a little cold...swallowed a little water, but okay."

He turned on the signal device then grabbed a watertight package, took out a blanket and wrapped it around her. Then he took one of the paddles and started for the island. Britt knew the coast guard would come for them very soon. Not only had he radioed their position, he had also activated the emergency signal in the floatation package. Once again he made sure Ashley was wrapped securely in the blanket then pulled her close to him, holding her next to his body.

He felt her shiver. "Are you sure you're okay?"

"I'm fine, honest." She felt the uncontrollable tremors start deep inside then quickly spread through her body. Now that it was over and they were both safe, the fear she had been valiantly trying to suppress came rushing to the surface. She could not stop shaking. She felt the tears slowly slide down her cheeks. "Britt, the plane—will you be in very much trouble with the charter company?"

He continued to hold her, rocking her gently in his arms. "The plane was mine, not the company's." His voice was flat, revealing no emotion of any kind.

He stared out at the spot where the plane had disappeared into the black depths of the ocean. It was the only plane he personally had ever owned. He had bought it when he was eighteen; his father had cosigned the loan. It had great sentimental value—but now it was gone.

He glanced down at Ashley. At least she was safe. That was more important than the plane. The realization slowly spread throughout his body, then quickly manifested itself as full-blown knowledge. Ditching the plane had brought more than shared danger into their lives. It had brought the unwelcome knowledge that she meant more to him than a potential bedmate and definitely more than just a casual friend. It was a bit of knowledge that truly frightened him. Every instinct told him to turn and run before it was too late.

The sound of the approaching coast guard rescue helicopter interrupted his thoughts. With quick precision they were transported back to the charter company office after refusing to be taken to the hospital.

When they entered the offices, Ellen jumped up from behind her desk. "Are you two all right? I heard the call on the radio."

"We're fine. I had to ditch the plane in the drink. It's now at the bottom of the Sound. I think it was a broken oil line. Would you take care of the paperwork for me?"

Ellen looked at him, her expression clearly showing how badly she felt for him. "Don't worry. And Britt...I'm very sorry."

He drove Ashley home and walked her to her apartment. She turned back toward him after unlocking her door and offered him a sincere smile. "I'll say one thing for sure, knowing you has been anything but dull. This has definitely been the most eventful and action-packed afternoon I've ever spent."

He was relieved to see her taking everything so well. She did not seem angry or upset. He offered a shy smile as he tried to hide his embarrassment. "You certainly haven't caught me at my best. First, you nurse me through the flu, then to show you my appreciation I crash-land you in the ocean.'' He looked into the turquoise depths of her eyes. ''Are you sure you're all right?'' He offered a shy smile. ''Do you think you'll ever speak to me again?''

''You aren't going to get off the hook that easily. You'll have to put up with me for a while longer.'' As soon as the words escaped her lips, she regretted having said them. They sounded too personal, too intimate, rather than just a friendly remark.

''Good.'' He kissed her on the cheek.

''Britt...'' The quiet moment made her sincere words sound much louder than they were. ''I'm very sorry about your plane.''

He ran his fingertips gently across her cheek and down the side of her neck as he spoke, his voice filled with the sorrow he felt. ''So am I.''

He was relieved at her lack of ill will toward him for what had happened. And her words that he would have to put up with her for a while longer thrilled him. He truly hoped it would be a lot longer.

5

Britt walked Ashley to her front door at the conclusion of a busy Friday. They had spent the day prowling through antique shops looking for a rolltop desk to put in his bedroom. It had been a carefree few days for both of them as they shared activities and solidified their friendship. They talked about their families, their backgrounds, and shared personal information, but neither of them had been able to share the extent of the pain resulting from their most recent relationships. That was a level of intimacy that each of them had left tucked safely away.

Ashley stood with her back against the closed door as he leaned forward, resting his hands on either side of her head. "I have a charter very early tomorrow morning, but I'll be back about four o'clock. I'd like to take you out to dinner tomorrow night, someplace very nice to celebrate the start of your new job Monday morning."

He leaned his face very close to hers, tilted his head to one side and then hesitated, not sure how to proceed. His dilemma of just what and how much she meant to him had not been far from the forefront of his consciousness since the plane crash. After a moment he kissed her, but not the kiss he wanted to give her. It was another casual brushing of her lips. "What about my dinner invitation?" He was afraid to say *date*, afraid of what it implied.

"It sounds great. I'd love it."

"Good. I'll pick you up about seven o'clock tomorrow night." He gazed intently into her eyes for a long moment as his finger traced the outline of her lower lip. "Good night, Ashley."

"Good night, Britt."

Tremors raced through her body as she watched him enter his apartment, then she turned and unlocked her front door. Somehow—she was not sure exactly how or when the exact moment occurred—she had allowed herself to become emotionally involved with Britt Carlton. Maybe he was not aware of it, but she certainly felt it every time he came near her. The heat of her desire suffused her entire body every time he touched her, every time he bestowed one of those innocent little kisses of his.

She wished just once he would kiss her, *really* kiss her as if he meant it. On more than one occasion she had been very tempted to take the initiative, but at the last minute she always chickened out. She usually ended up chastising herself over her errant and totally inappropriate thoughts. She knew exactly what he was and what he represented. She had been down that road before and it was a trip she did not want to make again. He was a womanizer who was the wrong man for her. In fact, he was probably the wrong man for any woman who wanted a commitment and expected a future with him.

A slight wrinkle of confusion furrowed her brow. Her argument was getting old…fast. She reminded herself that since *she* had spent so much time with him over the past three weeks he could not possibly be seeing anyone else. She also knew, his teasing aside, that he had behaved with the utmost propriety and consideration. She should have felt relieved, but for some unsettling reason she was not. She had to admit that she wished the bad boy she knew

was inside Britt would finally come out of hiding and
show himself for what he was.

Britt had just finished making dinner reservations for
the following night when his doorbell rang. A broad smile
came to his face as he walked briskly to the door, thinking
that it could be no one other than Ashley.

"Britt!" Julie said breathlessly as she walked into his
apartment, closing the door behind her. She reached her
hand to the top button of his shirt. "Where have you been
keeping yourself? Every time I've stopped by to see you,
you've been out." She began unbuttoning his shirt as she
pressed her body against his. "I was beginning to think
you were avoiding me."

He grabbed her hands as she unfastened the second
button on his shirt. "This really isn't a good time. I have
a flight early in the morning, and I need my sleep."

She freed her hands from his grasp, then pulled his
shirttail out of his jeans. "But, sweetie, all I want to do
is help you relax. Besides, I'm going back to Phoenix
tomorrow. This is our very last opportunity to get together." She smiled seductively as she ran her hands up
under his shirt and across his bare chest.

His voice faltered as he tried to regain control of the
situation. "Really...I have to get up very early in the
morning." He swallowed hard and took a calming breath
before firmly grabbing her elbow and ushering her out the
front door. "You'll have to run along."

Britt quickly closed the door and leaned back against
it. He drew in a calming breath as he refastened the shirt
buttons Julie had undone. She was definitely not his type,
but his shaken state told him how close he had come to
allowing himself to succumb to the temptation. Had it not
been for Ashley he might have done just that. He had

been alone for too long, yet the thought of being with someone other than Ashley did not appeal to him. He took another calming breath in an attempt to draw some comfort from the image of Ashley that had popped into his mind.

Ashley was putting the last of her dinner dishes in the dishwasher when her routine was interrupted by a knocking on her balcony door. She grabbed a towel and dried her hands before pulling open the sliding glass door so Britt could come inside.

"Hi, come on in. Weren't you going to go to bed early so you could get plenty of rest for your flight in the morning?"

He went to her without uttering a word, put his arms around her and pulled her to him—holding her tightly with his cheek resting against the top of her head. He could feel her soft warmth pressed against him. He inhaled the subtle fragrance of her perfume, the scent bringing to mind a hazy memory of a sensual delight nestled in his hand.

Ashley did not know what to do. There was something so very genuine about his actions. This was far removed from his normal kidding around. She tentatively reached her arms around him. She sensed his need for some sort of closeness, a comforting hand.

"Britt?" Her words were clouded with confusion. "Is something wrong?" He continued to hold her without speaking. A note of concern tinged her voice. "Are you okay?" He continued to hold her without saying anything. Anxiety seeped into her consciousness. She did not know what to do or how to respond.

He finally released her from his embrace. He took a step back and looked into her eyes as his fingers ligly traced her jawline then trailed down the curve of her neck. After a long moment he spoke, his voice filled with an aching emptiness. ''I'm sorry, I didn't mean to disturb you. I had an overwhelming need to touch reality.''

He enfolded Ashley in his arms again, molding her against his body. This time it was more of a caring, warm hug, as the frantic urgency of a few minutes earlier seemed to have disappeared. ''Sorry. I didn't mean to...well, whatever it is you thought, I didn't mean to.''

''That's okay, I guess. Whatever it is you meant.'' Bewilderment clouded her thoughts. ''Britt? What are you talking about? You have me totally confused.'' She stepped back and looked into his silvery gray eyes and tried to read his thoughts and feelings. In an instant she saw a wall go up as his expression changed from one of emotion to the easy camaraderie she'd come to expect from him.

''You're confused? Why don't you come home with me and I'll see if I can straighten you out?'' he teased.

''Come home with you! I thought you had an early flight and were going to bed.''

He flashed her a mischievous grin. ''I *am* going to bed early...want to join me? That's where I do some of my best *straightening out.*''

His words startled her. She was not sure how to interpret them. Perhaps it was her uncertainty about the nature of her own thoughts where Britt was concerned that had created her inner turmoil. She finally decided to treat his comments as just another joke. She flashed him a teasing grin. ''I think I'll pass this time. Thanks for asking, though.''

''You might want to reconsider. After all, this is a limited-time offer. You could be missing the opportunity of a lifetime.''

He stood back and looked at her, the little-boy grin slowly fading from his face. "You don't seem to be treating this offer with the proper amount of respect." He looked deeply into her eyes as he gently cupped her face in his hands. His voice turned soft, his words cloaked in an undeniable sincerity. "I'm really quite serious."

She frantically searched his face for some clue indicating what kind of game they were playing. She had become comfortable with the open, easy banter between them. But this—she did not recognize this new tact. She felt confused and uncertain how to handle this new line of kidding. It was only kidding...right?

He saw the look in her eyes and realized he had gone too far. She was not the type of woman who would jump into bed with a man just for the sole purpose of recreational sex. For Ashley there would have to be much more, certainly more than what he was able to offer. A quick image of Ashley standing at her front door wearing her robe and a man leaving her apartment pushed its way into his consciousness, but he refused to give it consideration. Whatever had been going on, well...part of him wanted to know about it, but the other part was afraid of what the truth might be.

He made an attempt to ease her obvious discomfort by laughing, an easy warm laugh. "You should see the look on your face. I've never seen such a muddled expression on someone who claims to be a mature adult of reasonable intelligence."

She immediately felt relieved at his change in attitude. And the tension churning inside her stomach was assuaged. "You'd be enough to muddle anyone. Now, why don't you go home and let me finish doing my dinner dishes?"

"Sure thing, see you tomorrow night." He kissed her on the forehead, then left.

After Britt's departure, Ashley sat on the couch lost in thought. The past three weeks had been so much more than she ever thought they would be, especially given her considered opinion of the life-style Britt represented and the type of man she believed him to be. Their time together had been a pure joy. Even the dumping in Puget Sound had not dampened her enthusiasm.

She tried to force the thought that Britt really was not at all like her ex-fiancé, but it was no good. She knew she was making excuses for Britt, rationalizing his behavior, both physical and emotional—clearly a sign that she had already crossed the line that separated simple friendship from involvement. They were not lovers…yet. But it was a very real possibility that hovered just on the other side of the hill. She knew that just as surely as she knew he could end up breaking her heart if she allowed her emotions to become involved in the same way as her desires were.

In that regard she knew he was exactly like her ex-fiancé. Marriage, home and family would never be part of Britt's plan for the future. He would always end up feeling restless and confined. He would ultimately need to move on to new things…and new people. He was the type who would eventually resent the person he felt had trapped him in a relationship. Some men simply were not the marrying kind, and Britt Carlton was one of those men.

Every time she thought of Britt she vividly recalled his touch—his fingers brushing her nipple, his hand… A shiver moved up her spine as an anxious, restless need consumed her—an unresolved need that fully occupied her consciousness whenever they were apart. A longing, a yearning, a desire to be with him constantly.

An involuntary laugh forced its way out of her throat. If the idea was not so preposterous, she would think she was falling in love with him. Her body jerked to attention. She sat rigidly on the edge of the couch and felt her eyes widen in shock.

It was a conscious thought she had been trying desperately to avoid, a conscious thought that unnerved her. Putting words to her emotional turmoil was the last thing she wanted to do, especially when one of those words was *love*.

To admit to herself that she might be falling in love with Britt Carlton was a betrayal of all her plans and choices for the future. A man like Britt Carlton would never be able to settle down, would never be satisfied with only one woman, would never want to get married and raise a family. No...to be in love with Britt Carlton was unthinkable and totally unacceptable.

She suddenly realized what starting her new job on Monday would mean. They would be apart all day long, five days a week. The separation would be good. It would give her time for her feelings to cool down and reason to prevail.

In his own apartment, in his large, lonely bed, sleep eluded Britt. He lay wide awake, his mind filled with tantalizing thoughts about Ashley Thornton. Of late, she was almost all he thought about—the fun they had, the serious moments they shared, the warm glow he felt whenever she was around, the wild surges of excitement that raced through his body whenever he touched her. He fought the slight smile that tried to turn the corners of his mouth. If he did not know better, he would almost believe he was falling in love with her.

His body jerked to attention. He sat rigidly upright in

bed. The conscious thought unnerved him. Putting words to his emotional turmoil was the last thing he wanted to do. To admit to himself that he was falling in love with Ashley Thornton was a betrayal of everything he had so carefully erased from his life. Love did not fit into his neatly closed off and self-contained future. A woman like Ashley Thornton would expect a full commitment in a relationship, and that meant marriage. She deserved no less. But it was the one thing he could not offer—not now and not ever. He had been burned before. To try again was unthinkable.

Before she knew it, Ashley was dressing for her dinner date with Britt. *Date*—the word made her uncomfortable. From the very beginning she had told herself it was okay to be friends with someone like Britt Carlton, but never to become seriously involved with that type of man again. Up until now she had not thought of the time they had spent together as actually dating. She tried her best to rationalize getting dressed up and going to a very nice restaurant as being just one more casual evening spent with a friend. But still, her insides quivered with the mixed feelings and emotions about their *non*date.

The clothes hanging in her closet seemed to stare back at her as she studied her choices. There was the red chiffon dress or the turquoise crepe de chine. She reached for the turquoise crepe. She had been to the beauty shop that afternoon for a manicure, pedicure, shampoo and set—the whole works. Her hair had been styled in an upswept manner, very attractive and flattering to the shape of her face.

After she finished dressing, she studied her reflection in the mirror. The crepe dress accentuated her waist with the neckline showing just a hint of cleavage. She completed her ensemble by slipping her feet into a pair of high heels the exact same shade as her dress. A gold necklace with a single diamond pendant graced her neck with matching gold and diamond earrings. The set had been a college graduation present from her parents. And impulsively she had added a touch of gold glitter to her glossy dark hair. She believed she was now ready.

No sooner had Britt arrived home than he laid out his clothes for the evening—a three-piece charcoal pin-striped suit, a pale blue shirt with French cuffs and a gray-and-blue-patterned silk tie. His dark gray Gucci loafers had been polished and buffed to a high sheen. A pair of monogrammed gold cuff links and a very stylish, thin gold watch completed the look.

He wanted tonight to be special. No matter what he said or consciously thought, he knew tonight was different from the casual outings they had been enjoying together. He felt as jittery as a schoolboy on a first date. *Date.* The word caused his throat to constrict. Dating had not been part of their friendship so far. Tonight, however, was different and he knew it. What he did not know was what to do about the uncertainty that jittered inside him.

He did a final check of his appearance, took a calming breath to fight down his anxiety, then left his apartment.

When Ashley opened her front door, he let out a long, low whistle of appreciation. He could not stop the smile from slowly spreading across his face as his eyes traced the outline of her curves. His heart beat faster and his mouth felt dry. The thought that lodged in his mind and screamed in his ear told him he could very well be in a great deal of trouble. Did he have enough willpower to keep his hands off her for the entire evening? He returned his gaze to her face, to her beautiful turquoise eyes, and thought about how perfect she was, how tantalizingly close—how incredibly desirable.

Ashley's voice cut into his wandering thoughts. "Do you prefer to stand outside with that silly grin on your face or would you like to come inside?" He looked too handsome and sexy for words. As he stepped through the door, he placed his hands on her shoulders and leaned forward to kiss her on the cheek.

"You look ravishing!"

"Thank you, sir." She gave him a dazzling smile as she ran her fingers along the lapel of his suit coat. "You look pretty terrific, too."

He held his hand up in the air and moved it in a circular motion. "Come on, turn around…let me see how you look from all angles."

Her quivering insides told her she should have chosen the red dress. Unfortunately she was committed to what she quickly realized had been a gross error in judgment. "Are you sure you're ready for this?" Her voice held just a hint of hesitation.

As soon as she turned away from him, he knew exactly what she meant. The dress was backless. The soft fabric went from her shoulders straight down to the waistband. He reached out his hand. His slightly trembling index finger lightly traced the outline of her dress from her shoulder down to her waist, across her waist to the other side and back up to the opposite shoulder. His breathing became labored; his mouth felt like cotton.

The sensation of Britt's finger lightly moving across her bare skin was almost more than her sensibilities could absorb. She felt a tingle start deep within and build as it moved outward—a feeling of panic accompanied by a very warm glow that was both sensual and soft. She shoved away the sensations as she turned to face him.

What she saw in his expression sent a jolt of electricity through her body. His silver eyes had turned a dark, smoldering gray; his face held a look of intense sexuality. Their eyes remained locked for a long moment as the very air around them seemed to sizzle. She tried to swallow, to ease the dryness in her mouth and throat.

With great difficulty Britt broke the spell that seemed to be binding them together. He did not like the hint of huskiness he heard as he spoke. "Dinner reservations are for seven-thirty. We'd better be going or we'll be late." He managed a weak smile, trying to project a casual manner. "Do you have a wrap of some sort?"

Ashley handed him the evening coat that matched her dress, then they left.

After what seemed like the longest car ride of their lives, Britt and Ashley were seated in a quiet corner of an elegant restaurant, well-known for its superb cuisine and excellent service. The table setting included fine linen, bone china, sterling silver and crystal. Each table held the extra touch of candlelight and fresh flowers.

A distinct and uncomfortable awkwardness presented itself, one that had not previously existed between them. Britt feigned an avid interest in the wine list. Ashley forced her gaze away from him and around the room before picking up the menu and pretending to study the selections.

She tried to swallow her mounting tension and anxiety. Her logic of whom and what she knew him to be seemed to be buried under her overwhelming desire for the man seated across the table from her—a man she knew was wrong for her in every sense of the word.

"Why don't I order a bottle of champagne and some appetizers? We can decide on dinner a little later. What would you like?"

"I'm sure I'll like whatever you choose. But please...no raw squid or octopus," she added, as an afterthought.

His mischievous grin turned the corners of his mouth. "Well, there go my first two choices."

His teasing and her spontaneous laugh broke the tension, and things immediately settled into the relaxed and comfortable mode that each had come to know and expect. They looked at each other and burst out laughing again. It seemed they each had exactly the same thought—they were glad the awkward moments had passed and things had returned to *normal.*

After they'd enjoyed an excellent meal, Britt helped her with her coat as they waited for valet parking to bring the car around. "If you're not too tired, I have part two of the evening planned. Are you game?"

She looked questioningly at him. "What do you have planned?"

"No fair answering a question with a question. You're either game for part two or you're not. Which is it?"

She looked into his eyes and saw the teasing twinkle she had come to know so well. "Why not? Lead on."

He took her to a small club that featured soft music and dancing—the kind of music, as Britt said, where you could dance without feeling as if you had been through an aerobics class.

He led her out on the dance floor and drew her to him as he started moving to the music. She fell in easily with his rhythm and movements. It felt as if they had been dancing together for years, they were so in sync. She rested her head against his shoulder as he put his cheek against the top of her hair. It seemed the most natural thing for them to be doing.

The sensations of his touch completely enveloped her;

his hand felt warm and exciting against her bare back, and his fingers moved sensually across her skin, leaving fiery trails in their wake. His body felt hard and strong, yet he was gentle and tender.

Britt held her, barely aware of the music playing or the other people on the dance floor. She felt so soft, so warm, so right in his arms. He wanted to stay just as they were forever—suspended in time, nothing and no one except the two of them.

But, of course, the evening had to come to an end. It was very late when he walked Ashley to her apartment. He took the key from her hand and unlocked the door. "Ashley..." His voice trailed off as he cupped her chin in his hand and gazed at her incredible turquoise eyes, her delicious-looking mouth.

Ashley felt herself being drawn into his aura, surrendering herself to his magnetism. She barely had enough breath to force out the word. "Yes?"

"Ashley..." He lowered his mouth to hers, tasting the sweetness of her lips.

She placed her hand on his cheek, her fingertips brushing against the bits of glitter that had transferred from her hair to his skin while they were dancing. She briefly returned his kiss, then pulled her head back from him. She searched his face and looked into his eyes, sensing an intense hunger about him, an unfulfilled emptiness. The realization startled her. It was not what she had expected. In an anguish-filled voice she responded to his unspoken desire from a place of panic rather than from her own desire. "Britt, this can't happen. I...it can't."

"I know." He spoke very softly, almost an inaudible whisper. He took one step back, his eyes never losing contact with hers. "I know." He brushed his lips lightly against hers. "Good night, Ashley."

She saw longing mixed with a deep sadness as she held his gaze. Her insides churned with emotional turmoil, the soft sensuality of his brief kiss emblazoned on her mind. There was nothing she could do but go inside and let him go home. "Good night, Britt."

Sleep eluded her as she tried to escape the reality of her torment. She stared up at the ceiling. Her body ached for his touch. She turned over and pounded her pillow into a comfortable shape, trying to find a position that would allow her to go to sleep.

The entire evening had been wonderful—the dinner was exquisite, the dancing marvelous and the kiss at her front door magical. In fact, it had been much more than wonderful. It had been the most enchanting evening she had ever spent with a man. Britt made her heart pound, her pulse race and sent tremors of joy coursing through her body. He made her feel very special. She could not imagine life without Britt Carlton.

She frowned, shook her head in dismay, then let out a sigh of resignation. She had better be able to imagine life without Britt Carlton because that was how it would ultimately be. He was just another philandering charmer who took his pleasures, then moved on to the next conquest. She closed her eyes, forcing her body to relax and her mind to stop creating images of what could never be.

Britt was not having an easier time of it than Ashley was. He had never felt such total frustration in his life. He paced anxiously up and down his bedroom floor. He wanted her totally, completely and forever. One date would not be enough, a thousand would not be enough. The realization had been difficult for him to deal with on a conscious level. The reality of his thoughts scared him more than anything had ever frightened him in his life.

He climbed back in bed and pulled the covers up across

his chest. His thoughts retraced the events of the evening they had just spent together—the dress that had almost taken his breath away, the flickering candlelight playing across her beautiful face at dinner, the warmth of her body nestled in his arms on the dance floor and the sweetness of her lips as he kissed her good-night.

Then the memory of her words lodged itself in his consciousness. *Britt, this can't happen.*

He finally drifted into an uneasy sleep.

6

Ashley remained in bed even though she had been awake for quite a while. Her night's sleep had been anything but restful. That made two nights in a row she had not slept well, and both were attributable to Britt Carlton. Not only did he seem to consume her waking thoughts, now he had invaded her sleep, as well.

She grabbed her robe as she reluctantly slid out from under the covers. She quickly made the bed back into a couch and straightened the room. After taking a shower and getting dressed, she gathered her dirty clothes and headed for the laundry room.

She was just removing some items from the dryer when Britt burst through the door, juggling his laundry basket and box of detergent.

Britt's entire spirit lifted the second he spotted her. He allowed a mischievous grin to slowly spread across his face as he casually sauntered over to where she stood. He raked his gaze across the neatly folded lingerie in her laundry basket, finally settling on the numerous pairs of lacy bikini panties. He winked at her. ''Need any help with those?''

He set his basket on top of one of the washers, then reached into her basket and picked up a pair of sheer, black panties. He held them up to the light, then allowed his gaze to slowly travel up her body until their eyes met. "I'll bet you look real sexy in these," he teased, his voice soft and sensual.

She returned his jest with a sly grin. "Not any more than you do in those bright red briefs you own."

He felt a rush of heat spread across his cheeks and neck as he recalled his recent bout of the flu. He quickly tried to regain the upper hand. "You've seen me in those, but I've never seen you in these." His voice dropped to a seductive whisper. "Would you like to model them for me sometime?"

She held his look for a long moment as she made a conscious effort to maintain their light banter. *Would she like to model them for him sometime?* You bet she would...sometime, anytime, perhaps now. She quickly grabbed the panties from him, their hands touching briefly. She returned them to her laundry basket, then picked up her box of detergent. "Only in your dreams, fella. Only in your wildest dreams."

Her touch lingered against his skin. She was always in his dreams—his daydreams and his night dreams and everything in between. She filled his every thought. A quick surge of panic darted through him as he watched her gather her laundry to leave. He did not want her to go. "What do you have planned for the rest of today? After laundry, that is."

"First, I have ironing to do and then housecleaning. I have carpets to vacuum, floors to mop, a kitchen and bathroom to clean and furniture to dust and polish."

"Ugh! Sounds awful. I have a cleaning lady come in once every other week to do all that. Of course, now that you made me buy all that new stuff for my apartment, she'll probably want to charge me more money." He grinned at her as his gaze slowly wandered across her face then settled on her eyes.

"Well, some of us are in a more financially secure position than others. You have to remember that I haven't had a paycheck for a month. Tomorrow my new job starts, and once again I can feel like a contributing member of society." She picked up the basket containing her folded laundry and turned toward the door. "I'd better get busy if I expect to get everything done today. I'll see you later."

"Yeah…see you later." He watched as she left the laundry room. He, too, had things to do. For the past three weeks he had neglected his job. He had only flown three charters. He needed to go to his office and check the schedule for the upcoming week.

Monday morning found Ashley up early, preparing for her first day at work. The prospects of her new job excited her. She had liked Stuart Billington very much when she met with him. He was a soft-spoken yet very dynamic man of about fifty with dark hair, graying at the temples. His office had a warm, comfortable feel about it. A framed photograph of his wife and three children rested on his desk.

She took extra care with her hair and makeup and left her apartment fifteen minutes earlier than she had originally planned. She was not sure how much time it would take to drive to her office in the morning rush-hour traffic, and she did not want to take a chance on being late her first day.

She was at her desk, familiarizing herself with some of the current project files when Stuart Billington entered the office. His smile was warm and gracious. "Good morning, Ashley. Are you getting settled in okay?"

She returned his smile. "Good morning, Mr. Billington. Yes, I'm finding everything I need, thank you."

"You can drop the *Mr.* if you'd like. Just call me Stu. We're very informal here. It makes for a more relaxed working atmosphere, and I believe a relaxed working atmosphere makes for greater productivity."

"Thank you. Stu it is, then." She stacked the folders she had been reading and placed them on the edge of her desk. "Is there any particular place you would like me to begin?"

"Yes. The timing is perfect. Your arrival exactly co-incides with a new project I'm putting together. We can both commence on the ground floor with this one. Why don't you come into my office and I'll brief you on what I've done so far." Stu walked to his office and Ashley followed. "We'll be dealing primarily with Al Canton in Los Angeles and Ed Simpson in Denver. I'm real excited about this deal."

The rest of the day flew by. Ashley had been very busy, totally engrossed in her new assignment. Before she knew it, the clock read six, and she was already an hour late leaving the office. When she entered Stu's office, he was still at his desk hard at work.

"Is there anything you need before I leave for the day?"

He looked up from the numerous files on his desk and offered a weary smile. "No, not a thing. Thanks for staying late. I think we really accomplished a lot, especially for your first day on the job. I know how tough it is to throw yourself into a new project when you haven't even found out where the bathrooms are or where we keep the coffeepot."

Stu rose from behind his desk and walked across the office toward her, his expression warm and gracious.

"You did a terrific job today. It's a real pleasure to have you as part of the organization. See you in the morning."

She felt her cheeks flush in response to his compliments. "Thanks, Stu. Good night."

As soon as she got home, Ashley changed into jeans and her football jersey. She fixed a quick dinner for herself. Just as she placed the last dish in the dishwasher, she heard Britt knock at her balcony door. She hurried to let him in.

He kissed her lightly on the cheek as he entered her living room, pulling the sliding door closed behind him. "Well...tell me. How was your first day at work?"

Her face lit up with enthusiasm as she began to tell him about her new job. Her excitement filled the room with an energy that quickly enveloped him. It was the same type of sparkle she had shown when they had gone sightseeing. It was the same fresh, open honesty that he had found so appealing the first time she displayed it.

"Oh, my. I've been babbling on and on and haven't even offered you anything. Would you like a glass of wine?"

"Can't. I have to fly tomorrow morning. In fact, I'll be gone for the next three days." He reached into his pocket and withdrew a key. "Here." He pressed it into her hand, a pleading little grin on his face. "This is the spare key to my apartment. Could you water all those plants for me?"

She closed her fingers over the key. "Sure, I can do that. Where are you going?"

"New York and then Boston. I'll be back Thursday night." He placed his fingers under her chin and raised her face. He plumbed the depths of her turquoise eyes as his index finger traced her lower lip and jaw before trailing down the side of her neck. "I'm going to miss you."

His voice was soft, containing just a hint of sensuality as he spoke. He continued to look into her eyes. "Could we have dinner Friday night or maybe go to a movie?"

She felt the full force of his presence. His touch caused tremors of delight. "It would be a pleasure." Her breathing quickened. She dared not say anything more for fear her quavering voice would give away too much of what was going on inside her.

"Good. I'll check with you when I get back Thursday night." He returned his fingers to the underside of her chin. His gaze lowered to her mouth as her pink lips parted slightly. Against his own conscious will, he slowly lowered his head, his mouth closing over hers. He briefly tasted the sweetness of her mouth, felt the softness of her lips.

No! He knew he couldn't—shouldn't—start anything. He drew back his head and released her chin from his grasp. He took a couple of awkward steps toward the patio door. "I'd better be going. I have to be up pretty early."

Once again Ashley felt herself being drawn into the energy of his aura, something she seemed helpless to prevent. She was grateful that he had put a stop to the kiss. "I'm pretty tired, too. I'll water the plants for you and see you Thursday evening." She walked with him to the balcony door. "Have a good flight."

She watched as he hopped from her balcony railing to his, then went inside his apartment. Once again he had left her wanting more of the heat of his passion...the heat he infused her with every time he touched her. She felt as if she were on a never-ending roller coaster ride with each twist and turn more thrilling than the last. She feared what would happen if she stayed on the ride to its conclusion. Would Britt move on, leaving her with memories and nothing more? It was a prospect that truly frightened her. The line dividing friends and lovers became more obscure with each encounter. Could Britt Carlton somehow be both?

The next morning Ashley woke early, eager to start her workday. She thoroughly enjoyed her new job and liked her co-workers. Stu Billington was the ideal boss—intelligent, dynamic, a hard worker, but also fair and generous with his employees. She felt comfortable in her work surroundings and was pleased with the way her move to Seattle had turned out. But as her thoughts turned to Britt Carlton, feelings of uncertainty engulfed her. Along with feelings of anticipation.

Ashley kept busy with her new job while Britt was out of town, but she wasn't too busy to miss seeing him, if only to say hello. Finally Thursday arrived. Britt was due back that evening. A tremor of anticipation started gently and then rapidly increased as she drove home following a hard day at work. Pulling her car into the parking garage, she noticed Britt's parking space was still empty.

She picked up her mail from the lobby box and went to her apartment. After changing clothes, she settled down and opened the large envelope from her mother, containing several newspaper clippings her mother thought might be of interest to her, along with a note that said they were throwing a graduation party for her brother the upcoming Saturday night. Her immediate response to the news was disappointment. Her only brother was graduating from college, and she would not be there.

A light tapping on her balcony door interrupted her reading. Her heart beat a little faster as she hurried to open the drapes and unlock the door.

Britt stepped into the room, pulling the door shut behind him. How marvelous he looked, how much she had missed seeing him the past three days. He swept her into his arms and gave her a big hug as he kissed her on the cheek.

Britt felt so good having his arms around Ashley—to be touching her, holding her. He finally released her from his embrace and flashed a mischievous grin. "Well, tell me...did you miss me more than you could possibly say, or did you find someone else to occupy your time while I was gone?" The image of the young man leaving her apartment while she'd stood at the door in her robe flashed through his mind. He quickly shoved it aside before it could get a solid hold on his senses.

She had missed him more than she thought it was possible to miss anyone. She returned his grin and teased, "Don't flatter yourself. In fact, I've been so busy I didn't even realize it was Thursday already."

He lifted her chin until he could look directly into her turquoise eyes. He held her look for a long moment. "You don't really want me to believe that, do you?"

"No, I don't," she answered softly, her voice slightly husky. Her heart pounded, accompanied by tremors deep inside her body. She searched the silvery depths of his eyes. Each time she was around Britt, she felt less and less in control of her own emotions. She wanted him to hold her again, to kiss her—and, yes, to make love to her. The last thought she had been unable to suppress. It had grown too strong to be simply shoved from her mind as she had done in the past.

He continued to hold her gaze for what seemed to her like an eternity. Finally he encircled her in his arms and gently pulled her to him again, holding her closely. She responded by putting her arms around his waist and resting her head against his chest. It seemed the most natural thing to do. He stroked her hair as he nuzzled his cheek against the top of her head. Neither of them said a word as they stood together, their bodies gently pressed against each other.

After a long moment Britt spoke, breaking the silent spell that bound them together. It was a struggle for him to maintain his composure. He wanted to kiss her, to consume her mouth—to consume all of her. But that was not the way people behaved when they were just friends...nothing more. Reluctantly he released her from his arms, keeping hold of only her hand. She was so tantalizing, so tempting. "Have all my plants died yet?"

She laughed, but the tremors of excitement coursing through her body belied her casual exterior. "Don't be silly. You were only gone three days. Even *you* couldn't kill plants in only three days."

"You don't know my track record with plants." Only three days. It seemed so much longer. He led her over to the couch where they sat down. "Now, what's been happening with you?"

Her face lit up with enthusiasm as she began to tell him about the activities at her job. Her entire manner became animated as she continued to talk. "Oh, dear, I've been babbling again just like I did before. I guess I can't help it. I really like this job. I'm sorry to bore you with all of this."

He bent forward and kissed her on the forehead as he allowed a sincere smile. "I wasn't at all bored. I'm really glad you like your new job so much. I told you Stu Billington was a great guy. What else has been happening with you since I've been gone? Did you win the lottery or anything?" He gave her a quick wink. "Can you afford to take me away from all of this and support me in the manner to which I would like to become accustomed?"

"Nothing that exciting. I did get a letter from my

mother." Her mood reflected a touch of sadness. "There's going to be a graduation party for my brother this Saturday night. I'd really like to be there, but that's impossible."

He sat up straight, her words capturing his total attention. "Why is it impossible?"

"The cost of a last-minute airplane ticket is just too expensive. I can't afford full-fare coach to be in Wichita for only one day. It's out of the question."

"The cost of a plane ticket is the only obstacle?"

"Yes..."

A big grin spread across his face as he put his arms around Ashley and gave her a squeeze. His words burst out in an excited explosion. "Pack your bags and be prepared to leave immediately after work tomorrow. You're going to Wichita for that party."

Ashley looked at him as if he were crazy. "What are you talking about? How...I don't understand."

"The company just bought a new Cessna business jet. It's ready to be picked up at the plant in Wichita and ferried back to Seattle. It's a model that only requires one pilot rather than the two pilots that are usually necessary with a jet. I was going to give the job to someone else, but I just decided to pull rank and handle it myself. So, unless you're afraid to get in a plane with me again, I'm going to fly you. We can hop a ride with a buddy of mine who's flying a cargo charter Friday evening and bring the jet back on Sunday."

Her eyes grew wide as the reality of what he was saying got through to her. "Are you serious? You can really do that?"

"You bet I can—and will. Now you pack your bag and I'll take you to work in the morning. That way I can pick you up as soon as you get off and we can go directly to the airfield.''

"I don't know what to say." Her voice turned to an emotional whisper. Her eyes glistened as she blinked several times in an effort to keep the tears of happiness from trickling down her cheeks. She looked up at him. "Is this for real? You're not teasing me, are you?"

He looked into her moist eyes as he lightly brushed the hair back from her cheek with his fingers. He held her face in his hands as he continued to explore the depths of her turquoise eyes. "I've been looking for something special I could do to repay you for taking care of me when I had the flu—" a quick twinge of embarrassment darted through him "—and that little incident with the plane crash in Puget Sound." He softened his voice as a warm feeling overcame him. "You don't need to thank me. You don't owe me a thing. I'm the one who owes you."

Her voice was barely audible as she spoke. "I don't know what to say...." She looked deeply into the silvery gray depths of his eyes and was startled by what she saw. Desire? Intense passion? Was it real, or was she only wishing it to be so? Did she dare trust her feelings and desires rather than her experience? "Britt?"

"Yes…" His breathing had quickened as sensual stirrings raced through his body, settling deep inside him. He lowered his head to hers, preparing to kiss her. At the very last moment he avoided her lips, kissing her cheek instead. A sudden fear engulfed him. What if she thought he expected her to go to bed with him as payment for flying her to Wichita? The concern stopped him from doing any more than kissing her cheek. He spoke in a soft whisper. "I'd better get home. I have a suitcase to unpack and another one to pack." He ran his fingertips along her upper lip and across her cheek. "What time do you want to leave for work in the morning?"

She tried to hide her disappointment at his unexpected decision to go home. "About seven-thirty will be fine."

"Good. I'll see you in the morning, suitcase in your hand." He looked longingly into her eyes one more time. "Good night, Ashley." He reluctantly walked to the balcony door.

"Good night, Britt." She watched him leave her apartment. An aching emptiness settled in the pit of her stomach as he closed the sliding balcony door behind him.

Ashley rose early the next morning, packed a bag and prepared for her weekend trip. While waiting for Britt to pick her up at seven-thirty, she phoned her parents and told them about him flying her to Wichita that night then back to Seattle on Sunday.

"Now, Mother, please don't say anything to Bobby about me being at the party. I want to surprise him. I don't know what time we'll be getting into Wichita. I'm not even sure where we'll be landing, at the airport or at Cessna. Either way, we'll be on the west side of town, so it won't take you long to get there to pick us up. I'll just have to call you." Before she hung up, her mother insisted that Ashley invite Britt to stay at their house.

Her workday was very busy, but not so busy as to prevent her mind from wandering to the weekend. Her pleasure about the trip, of being able to see her family again, kept her in a constant state of excitement. But what excited her even more was that she would be spending the time with Britt.

Five o'clock finally arrived, and she cleared off her desk in preparation to leave. She raised her head and looked toward her office door in response to the sound of someone knocking. Britt stood framed in the doorway.

"Hi." The sound of his smooth masculine voice broke the silence in the room.

She felt a warm glow deep inside as she answered his greeting. "Hi, yourself."

"Britt, what a surprise." Stu Billington interrupted their private moment as he walked past Ashley's door. "What are you doing here?"

Britt turned to face Stu, the two men shaking hands as Britt replied, "I'm here to pick up Ashley."

Stu turned his attention to her. "You two know each other?"

She smiled shyly. "Yes. We're next-door neighbors."

"This is one great lady," Stu said, his comments directed toward Britt. "I don't know how I functioned in this office before she came to work here."

He started down the hall, then paused and turned around. Stu looked at Ashley and then Britt. An odd expression briefly crossed Stu's face, but was quickly replaced by a smile. "Well, you two kids have a good time." He turned toward Ashley. "I'll see you Monday morning. Good night."

Britt returned his attention to Ashley. "Are you ready to fly? No misgivings or apprehension?"

"Ready when you are."

He took her hand. "Let's go."

The cargo plane touched down at the Wichita airport on the west side of town. Britt waved toward the plane and smiled as he called out, "Thanks for the lift, Jack. I'll return the favor."

"Let me know next time you have something headed

for Hawaii. Barbara has been after me to take her somewhere.''

''You've got it. I'll give you a call.''

Ashley phoned her parents with instructions for where to pick them up. ''Fortunately, my folks live on the west side of town,'' she told Britt. ''They should be here in a few minutes.''

Before long, a man and a woman in their early fifties pulled up to the building where Ashley and Britt waited. ''Mother, Daddy!'' She threw her arms around both of them. Britt stood by, silently watching the excitement on her face and delighting in her happiness.

She caught a glimpse of Britt out of the corner of her eye and turned toward him. ''Mother...Daddy...I want you to meet Britt Carlton. Britt, this is my mother, Marilyn, and my father, Mike Thornton.''

Britt shook hands with Marilyn as he flashed her one of his best smiles. ''I can see where Ashley gets her good looks.'' He held up his hand to stop her from saying anything. ''I know, that sounds like empty flattery. On this occasion, however, it happens to be true.'' He turned his attention to Mike and extended his hand. ''Mike, it's a pleasure to meet you. Ashley tells me you're general manager of a radio station. My sister works for a radio station in Dallas.'' He directed his gaze at both of them. ''I certainly appreciate your inviting me to stay at your home. It's very kind of you to take in a total stranger, especially on such short notice. I'll try not to be too much of a bother to you.''

''It's small compensation, considering you're the one who made it possible for Ashley to be here,'' Marilyn responded. ''I'm sure you'll be no bother at all.''

''We're very happy to have you,'' Mike agreed. He

turned and headed toward the car. ''We'd better get going.''

Ashley could tell that Britt had instantly ingratiated himself with her parents. They were totally captivated by him. She was very pleased they had taken to him so quickly.

A short while later the car pulled into the garage of a large, one-story house. A brief tour revealed a living room with fireplace, a dining room and a kitchen with breakfast nook. A covered patio stretched across the back of the house. There was a master bedroom suite with private bathroom plus three other bedrooms, a den and two more bathrooms.

Marilyn and Ashley showed Britt the guest room. ''This will be your room, Britt. I hope you'll be comfortable. There's a bathroom through this door, and please feel free to use the closet. After you've unpacked, join us in the living room.'' She turned to Ashley. ''Come on, darling, let's get you situated.'' The two women left Britt alone in the bedroom.

He surveyed his surroundings as he unpacked his bag. The house was nice, tastefully decorated, very warm and comfortable. It reflected the warm, outgoing type of people Ashley's parents were. It reflected the closeness they felt as a family. He felt a similar type of closeness with his own family, even though they had been separated geographically for a while. It was the type of closeness he had immediately experienced with Ashley—the type of closeness he had never felt with Joan.

After unpacking, Britt went to the living room where everyone had already gathered. Mike looked up as he entered. ''Britt, come and sit down. Could I get you something to drink? A glass of wine, a beer or perhaps something a little stronger?''

Britt looked at his watch. "Well, perhaps a glass of wine." It was late and he was tired. He did not really want much to drink. Even though he was not into his twelve-hour cutoff time before flying, he still liked to be extra cautious prior to taking the controls of a jet, especially when he did not have a copilot with him.

Marilyn, Mike, Ashley and Britt sat up until three in the morning talking and laughing. Britt felt very comfortable with Ashley's parents. Finally everyone agreed it was very late and time to go to bed.

Before leaving the living room, Marilyn said, "Britt, the coffee automatically comes on at six o'clock in the morning. The first person up is expected to help himself, not wait for the others. Just feel free to make yourself at home. Good night." She turned to Ashley and gave her a hug. "Good night, dear. It's so good to have you home again, even if it is only for a couple of days."

Mike rose from his chair and followed his wife out of the living room, stopping to shake hands with Britt as he left. "Thanks for bringing Ashley home for the weekend. Good night, Britt."

"Good night, Mike." Britt watched as Ashley's parents walked down the hall to their bedroom. He turned to Ashley and placed his hands on her shoulders. "Well, I suppose it's time we went to bed, too." He felt the flush rise on his cheeks as he caught the expression on her face. "Uh...what I meant to say is it's time we went to sleep...that is, went to our own rooms." Again he paused as embarrassment claimed him. "What I—well, you know what I meant."

She smiled at him, her reply soft and caring. "Yes, I know what you meant. Good night, Britt. Thanks again for making this possible. You have no idea how much I appreciate your doing this." She felt her lower lip quiver slightly, then her lips parted. Her gaze lingered on his face, then slowly wandered to his mouth.

His gaze dropped to her mouth, to her tantalizingly parted pink lips. His voice grew husky as he spoke. "I'm glad I was able to find something special to do for you. Very glad..." His voice trailed off as he slowly lowered his head, enfolding her in his arms. He brushed his lips against hers then brought his mouth fully down upon hers.

"Oh, Ashley, dear." Marilyn's voice called out from down the hall as a bedroom door opened. Britt immediately released her as she stepped back from his embrace, her lips on fire and her insides trembling from the all too brief encounter. "Bobby is due home early tomorrow afternoon."

"Okay, Mother. That sounds great. Good night."

"Good night, dear." The bedroom door closed once again.

Ashley seemed slightly embarrassed, but he could not tell if it was because of the kiss they had started or because of her mother's interruption. Either way, the moment was gone. He leaned forward and kissed her on the forehead. "Good night." Then each of them walked to their respective rooms.

7

Ashley lay in bed wide awake. Once again, thoughts of Britt were giving her a sleepless night. She knew in the very depth of her existence that he was wrong for her. He was just another charmer who would never settle down to a lasting relationship. He might be feeling something special for her now, but it would fade away when he met someone new and exciting to take her place.

Charming rogues did not make for good husbands. She allowed a moment of bittersweet reflection. They did not make good fiancés either. She was sure it had something to do with commitment. The moment the commitment was *official* was the same moment they started looking elsewhere. She had learned that lesson the hard way.

She also knew she ached to be in Britt's arms. The frustration was compounded by the knowledge that he lay just on the other side of the bathroom that connected the two bedrooms—so close to her, yet so far.

Britt felt equally restless, unable to sleep. He was not sure which bedroom belonged to Ashley, but he knew she was in the same house with him, sleeping not that many feet away from his bed. How he wanted to be with her, to be sharing her warmth. He wanted to make love to her more than he had ever wanted to with any other woman.

If only those words she had spoken to him were not burned into his memory: *Britt, this can't happen.*

She was the type of woman who needed commitment. She was the type of woman who deserved commitment…and someone who could give it to her. The idea of opening up his innermost feelings and once again allowing himself to expose that vulnerable place still frightened him. As much as he wanted her, he did not think he could handle the emotional side.

He lay on his back, staring through the darkness toward the ceiling. His body ached for her as she filled his every thought. The more he thought about her, the more he wanted her; the more he wanted her, the more aroused and alive his body became. He climbed out of bed and crossed the room. The night-light in the bathroom provided just enough illumination for him to see without switching on the overhead lights.

He turned on the faucet, filled his cupped hands with cold water and brought them up to his face, allowing the coldness to splash over his cheeks and forehead then run down his neck and onto his bare chest. He repeated the procedure several times until his face, neck and chest were completely wet. He stood for a moment, leaning forward with his hands resting against the countertop. The cold water had done nothing to dampen his burning desires.

Ashley was every bit as restless as Britt. She tossed and turned. All she could think about was Britt, the feel of his touch and the scorching sensation of his lips on hers. But, too many nagging questions persisted in the back of her mind. Who was Joan? What did Julie and Cindy mean to him? And why, whenever he got too close to her, did he suddenly back off? She thought she had read something in his eyes the previous night. Had she only imagined it?

She felt restless stirrings surging through her body. She

knew it was her desire to be with Britt; her want—no, her *need*—for him to make love to her. She yearned for the pleasure of their physical union, the euphoric ecstasy she knew would be the result of their lovemaking. She shook her head and sat up in bed. It was no good. She had to rid her mind of these thoughts. She climbed out of bed and walked toward the bathroom while straightening the soft oversize T-shirt she used as a nightgown, a T-shirt that used to belong to her brother before it became so worn that it was threadbare.

She opened the bathroom door. The unexpected sight of Britt standing on the other side of the door startled her. His well-defined physique, highlighted by the dim illumination of the small night-light, excited her senses. Her pulse rate took an immediate jump, and her breathing quickened.

Britt looked up at the interruption. At first he did not realize who stood at the door, then his eyes focused on Ashley. He straightened up, water dripping from his wet skin. His gaze slowly wandered down her body to her feet, then up again to her face. The large wrinkled T-shirt made her look like a fine china doll that needed to be carefully wrapped up and protected so she would not break.

Even in the extreme dimness of the room he could make out the curves of her body under the thinness of the shirt. Her nipples formed taut peaks and pressed against the fabric. His breathing quickened. He extended his hand and slowly brushed his fingertips across her lips, along her jawline and down the curve of her neck. He felt a tremor, but did not know if it was Ashley or him trembling with excitement. Perhaps it was both of them.

Ashley stood still, unable to move, as he reached out his hand and lightly drew his fingertips across her skin. She felt herself tremble under the sensations of his touch.

This unexpected encounter was much too tempting. She wanted to throw herself into his waiting arms. Instead, she tentatively reached out and touched his chest, her fingers lightly brushing through the feathery wisps of hair. She heard a groan, or more accurately she felt the rumble start deep inside his chest and climb to his throat.

She held no control over her own actions; her hand acted independently of her conscious will. Her entire body tingled with sensual desire. All he had to do was take her; there was no way she could resist him—no way she wanted to resist him. No matter how wrong he was for her, she knew making love with him could not be more right. She hoped it was not something she would live to regret.

Her touch nearly destroyed Britt's last vestige of control. He looked into the depths of her eyes. He saw a mixture of passionate desire and cautious restraint. The combination confused him; he did not know how to interpret it. He had never been in a position where he did not know how to proceed with a woman—with the possible exception of when he'd lost his virginity at the age of sixteen to an experienced older woman of seventeen.

The sexual tension that was pulling them together refused to release him from its magnetic force. He reached down and grabbed her around the waist, lifted her up and set her on the counter. He leaned forward, his palms flat against the countertop on each side of her hips. He was very close, his face almost touching hers. Finally, in a voice thick with unfulfilled desire, he spoke. "This isn't the time or the place. We can't...not here, not now."

"Britt? What's the matter? Every time we get close, you back off. I thought there was something very special building between us." She took a calming breath, almost afraid to ask the next question. "Was I wrong?"

"No, you're not wrong. You're not wrong at all. There is something very special between us, at least I feel something special." He paused, wrinkling his brow as he tried to collect his thoughts. Things were no longer as simple as they had been when they first met. He was not sure exactly when or how it happened, but the situation between them had gone beyond the boundaries of just being friends. He knew he had to tell her about Joan, but he did not know how to do it. He took her hand in his, kissed the back of it, then turned it over and kissed her palm. He put his arms across her shoulders, then laced his fingers behind her neck. He had not talked to anyone about Joan or his feelings about what had happened—not even his family. He wanted to tell Ashley, though. He wanted her to know.

"I haven't wanted to be seriously involved with anyone. For the past four years I've purposely avoided any emotional entanglements. I didn't want to take a chance on being hurt again."

With those words he opened the door to his inner turmoil. He pushed forward. "Four years ago, I was about to be married to a woman named Joan. One day she simply walked out on me without even a word and ran off to Las Vegas and married her old boyfriend. Two days later I received a letter from her telling me what she'd done." He paused to take a steadying breath. "After that, I was afraid to take any chances." He hesitated again, the next part being the most difficult for him. "If it was a relationship that needed any type of commitment, then I didn't want anything to do with it."

He shifted his weight from one foot to the other. After a long moment of silence, he continued. "Then you came into my life and everything seemed fine, as long as we were just friends. Then one evening, at your front door, I leaned forward to kiss you and you pulled back and said, 'This can't happen.'" He brought his hands to her shoulders, then cupped her chin in one hand. "At first I thought you meant that I was moving too fast, but later I didn't know what to make of it. All I could figure was that you only wanted to be buddies—you know, just friends. I didn't want to frighten you by being too aggressive, so every time I wanted you so badly I couldn't stand it, I'd end up pulling back."

He paused a moment to calm his inner jitters. He was not sure, but this just might be the most difficult thing he had ever done, exposing his vulnerability and risking her rejection. "Ashley, I'm confused. Why can't this happen? If you're feeling the same attraction between us that I'm feeling, then why can't this happen?" It had been so much easier at first, back when it had been a choice of emotion-free sexual conquest or friends. But now...now everything had changed. It wasn't planned and he certainly had not sought it out, but he could not deny that he had become emotionally involved. He searched her face for some kind of sign, some kind of answer to his dilemma.

She rested her hand against his cheek and he placed his hand on top of hers. She looked into his questioning eyes for a long moment while gathering her thoughts. Finally she spoke, carefully measuring her words. "I had an unhappy experience, too. I was engaged for a short time to a man who turned out to be more interested in seeing how many conquests he could make than he was in building a lasting relationship with me. The last thing I wanted was to have a repeat of that situation—" she felt the shiver move through her body "—to become involved with another man who could not make a commitment."

He was not sure how to respond to what she had said. His mind flashed to the incidents with Julie and the phone call from Cindy. It was easy to see how she would have jumped to conclusions about him. And she would have been right. Up until six months ago he would have had to admit that he did fit the description—but not anymore. Each day he had spent with Ashley Thornton had put him one day closer to the realization that he truly wanted someone special in his life, someone he could share the future with. And that special someone was Ashley.

She paused as she continued to look at the serious expression on his handsome face, his intensity illuminated by the dim light. She looked into his eyes. They were growing dark as they regained the smoldering energy of earlier. She held his eye contact for a long moment as a shiver moved through her body. Right or wrong did not matter; all that mattered was how much she wanted Britt Carlton.

Her voice was half pleading and half determination. "Britt, if you don't kiss me right now—and I mean *really* kiss me—well, I think I'm going to just die."

He managed an impish grin as he replied, "Never let it be said that I didn't do everything in my power to save a human life."

He leaned his face into hers and softly captured her mouth, his lips tasting her sweetness. She put her arms around his neck as she returned his tenderness. The kiss quickly exploded with the power of long-suppressed sensual desires, moving from gentle to tumultuous as he consumed her mouth. She sat perched on the very edge of the countertop, her body pressed tightly against his.

His tongue darted between her lips, exploring the hidden recesses of her mouth. He felt the sensation of her fingers snaking through his thick hair as she answered his sensual advance, her tongue twining with his. A low, growling moan escaped his throat as his hands caressed her back and shoulders.

She could neither describe nor explain the sensations that totally enveloped her. She only knew no one had ever made her feel the way he did. This had to be more than mere lust. He made her heart sing, her spirits soar and her life seem unbelievably perfect...and the feeling came from just seeing him, talking to him. None of it had any association with his incredibly sensual mouth, his electrifying touch or his overwhelming physical presence.

Britt's mind was lost in a cloud of sensual delight. Ashley's mouth was so sweet, so delicious. He simply could not get enough of the taste of her, the sensation of her tongue twining with his, the feel of her taut nipples through the thin fabric of her shirt as they pressed against his bare chest. He wanted to make love to her, more than anything he had ever wanted in his entire life. He wanted to scoop her up in his arms and carry her to his bed. He wanted to touch all of her, taste all of her, be one with her. And he wanted it to last forever.

His hands slid under her T-shirt, his fingers tickling across her silky smooth bare skin. A hazy memory started to crystallize in his mind. His hand moved up her rib cage; his fingers lightly brushed her taut nipple. He heard her sensual moan, felt her bare foot brush along the edge of his calf. He closed his hand over her breast.

His head jerked back from her, his senses alive with recognition. The hazy memory that had been haunting him had suddenly become very clear.

The suddenness of Britt's actions startled Ashley. She looked into his eyes, her breathing labored, her tone questioning his action. "Britt?"

His hand still caressed her breast; his fingers gently manipulated the hardened nipple as he buried his face in her hair. Finally he spoke, very softly and very carefully. "I've done this before, haven't I?" He waited a long moment, his hand still covering the swell of her compact breast. The sensation of her puckered nipple and her warm flesh nestled in his hand were now part of a total recall. He remembered cupping her bare breast while in a feverish condition as she lay in bed next to him.

"Ashley..." He looked into her eyes again, searching for the truth. Slowly he removed his hand and smoothed down her T-shirt. "Tell me what happened in my apartment that night I had the flu and you stayed with me. How did it come about that my hand was resting over your bare breast while we were both in my bed? I've had a fuzzy image in my mind ever since that night. I was never able to figure out if it was real or some sort of delightful fantasy. But just now, when I touched you, it became crystal clear. It wasn't a fantasy. It actually happened, didn't it?"

She took several deep breaths, trying to slow her ragged breathing. She placed her arms around his neck as he pulled her against his chest, his fingers twining in her hair. Finally she spoke. "Yes, you have done this before. It was just as you said. You were in a very feverish state, shivering cold and trying to get warm. You reached out from under the covers and grabbed my wrist, pulling me down on the bed. Before I knew what you were doing, you had me under the covers with you and had wrapped your arms around me. I think you were instinctively trying to use my body heat to help get warm. Your hands just sort of wandered up under my shirt. I pulled loose from you and slid out of bed, then the pharmacy arrived with your medication. After that, you calmed down and went to sleep."

She lifted her head and looked into his questioning

eyes. "That's all there was to it. I didn't see any reason to mention it. I was sure it had been a total accident and that you didn't even remember what happened." There was no reason for her to repeat the suggestive words he had mumbled.

A look of relief covered his face. "Thank goodness, that's all it was. I was so afraid I'd done something to upset or embarrass you."

She smiled at him. "No, nothing like that."

Their breathing had returned to normal, and their heated passions had cooled a little. Each knew they should go back to their own room and get some sleep. It was almost time to get up. But neither wanted to part from the other.

Finally it was Ashley who spoke. "Like you said, this is neither the time nor the place. So...as long as you promise me there will be a right time and place, I think we should go to our own rooms and try to get some sleep."

"That's easy for you to say. I, for one, don't think I'll be able to sleep a wink for the rest of the night. And as for a right time and place, you can stake your life on it." Britt's mischievous grin returned. "How about at twenty thousand feet with the plane on autopilot? What do you think?"

"I think our previous experience together in an airplane is more than enough excitement, even though your suggestion would certainly be more to my liking than being dumped in the ocean again." She inched closer to the edge of the counter. "Here, help me down off this ledge before I fall off."

He lifted her off the counter and placed her on the floor. As he let go of her, he couldn't resist trailing his hand down her backside and slipping it under her T-shirt to give her bare bottom a gentle caress. He quickly withdrew his hand. "Hey, you've got a cold rear end."

She rubbed her hands across the fabric of her shirt where it stretched over her bottom in an attempt to warm her skin. "You think that little touch felt cold on your fingers? You should have been the one whose bare bottom was perched on that cold ceramic tile. I think I might have a first-class case of frostbite."

His voice dropped to a throaty, seductive timbre. "Do you want me to kiss it and make it feel better?"

She looked at the desire and mischief in his eyes and allowed a smile to slowly curl the corners of her mouth. "I'll bet it just might help. Wanna try?"

"Now, now, now..." He held her at arm's length. "Don't toy with someone who's in a highly aroused state and barely holding his composure...unless you're serious."

She looked into his eyes. "I'm quite serious, but you're right—we'd best get some sleep," she said, her voice soft and filled with longing.

He enclosed her face in his tender touch and kissed her affectionately on the lips, again tasting the sweet promise of things yet to be. "Good night, Ashley."

Ashley walked into the kitchen at nine-thirty the next morning and headed straight for the coffee. She'd only had five hours of sleep, but felt fully rested and at peace with the world. She poured herself a cup of coffee and carried it outside to the patio to join her mother and father. She set her cup on the table. "Good morning, Mother. Good morning, Daddy." She looked out across the horizon. "It's a beautiful morning."

Marilyn reached across the table and patted her hand. "Ashley, dear, you look positively radiant. I...uh...I don't mean to pry into your personal life, but you and your young man…well, all your letters and phone calls are filled with 'Britt this' and 'Britt that.' I just thought there might be something you'd like to tell us, something involving your future plans."

Ashley chuckled as she leaned over and put her arms around her mother, giving her a little hug. "First of all, he's not 'my young man.' Britt and I are just friends."

Mike put down his paper and leveled a questioning look at his daughter. "I'd call it a lot more than 'just friends' when the man flies you halfway across the country just to attend a party. Yes, indeed. I'd call that much more than just friends."

She could see the teasing gleam in her father's eyes. "Oh, Daddy, you're beginning to sound just like Mother. Now both of you, stop it. If there's anything to announce, you'll be the first to know."

Marilyn patted her daughter's hand again. "Of course, dear."

A sound from the kitchen interrupted their conversation. Ashley looked up and saw Britt pouring himself a cup of coffee. She called to him, "We're out here."

Britt walked out to the patio, carrying his coffee. "Good morning, Marilyn…Mike." He turned to face Ashley as he set his coffee cup on the table. "Good morning, Ashley." His voice softened and his smile radiated his delight at seeing her.

Her features took on the same soft glow as she returned his greeting. Marilyn and Mike exchanged knowing glances. Ashley turned her attention to her father. "Daddy, may I borrow your car? I want to buy Bobby a graduation present."

Mike chuckled as he reached in his pocket. "Some things never change. I remember when you turned sixteen and got your driver's license. The first thing you wanted was the car keys. It hardly seems possible but in another couple of weeks you'll be twenty-six. Where does the time go?'' He handed her the keys.

Ashley turned toward Britt. "Do you want to come with me? We won't be gone long."

"Sure." He glanced at his half-full cup of coffee, then winked at her. "Are you ready to go now, or do I get to finish my coffee?"

Marilyn spoke up. "Britt, would you like some breakfast? That cup of coffee isn't very much."

He gave Marilyn one of his best smiles. "No, thanks. Coffee is all I need." He downed the last swallow and rose from his chair. He turned his attention to Ashley. "Shall we go?"

As soon as Ashley and Britt left, Mike placed his newspaper on the table and looked at Marilyn. She returned his knowing look. "Mike, did you see the way they looked at each other? It's just so obvious. He clearly adores her, and I've never seen Ashley so radiant. I'm so happy she found someone, especially after that unfortunate situation with Jerry Broderick." They both watched as Ashley and Britt pulled out of the garage.

Ashley braked at the corner stop sign. She was preparing to pull out onto the main road when Britt reached over and shifted the car into park, then took her hand in his.

"What are you doing?" She started to reach for the gearshift. "We can't park right in the middle of the street."

"There's not another car in sight. Who's going to know?" He leaned over and kissed her tenderly on the lips, then drew back slightly so he could look into her eyes. He cupped her chin in his hand as he spoke. "I didn't have an opportunity to give you a proper good morning. This still isn't proper, but it will have to do for now." He leaned forward and kissed her again. He reveled in her softness, the feel of her silky skin as he stroked her cheek.

Her mind reeled. Every time he touched her it was all she could do to keep control of her senses. She ran her fingers through his hair as she reached her arms around his neck. His lips pressing against hers caused all the sensations she felt the night before to race to the surface.

A honking car horn shattered the moment. She quickly glanced in the rearview mirror at the car behind them. "Well, so much for privacy." She put the car in gear, checked the oncoming traffic and pulled away from the stop sign.

Britt leaned back in the bucket seat with his palms pressed tightly against his thighs. His eyes were closed. "It's just as well. I was beginning to have thoughts... trying to remember back to my teenage days. Trying to remember how to make love in the back seat of a car." He opened his eyes and gave her a sly sidelong glance, his mischievous grin tickling at the corners of his mouth.

She tried to suppress a laugh. She never knew what he would say next. A grin slowly curled the corners of her mouth. "The back seat of a car?"

He laughed out loud, a warm open sound, as he reached for her hand. "Desperate times call for desperate measures!"

She grinned. "You're incorrigible. Have I ever told you that?"

"I believe you might have mentioned it once or twice...or three times...maybe even four times. But since you never asked me to stop, I can only assume you must love it.''

His words were more truthful than he knew. She did love the way he teased, the surprising little comments that he sprang on her at the most unexpected times. And that was not the only thing she loved. There was the man himself.

8

Marilyn, Mike, Ashley and Britt were just finishing lunch on the patio when a voice called from inside the house, "Hello...is anyone home?"

Ashley jumped to her feet as a big smile spread across her face. "That's Bobby." She turned to Britt, grabbed his hand and pulled him from his chair. "Come on, I want you to meet him." She rushed into the house, Britt closely behind.

"Bobby!" She ran to greet her brother.

"Ashley..." Bobby dropped his overnight bag on the floor and held his arms open to her. "What a surprise. This is great. I didn't think you'd be here." He wrapped her in a big hug and kissed her cheek. He let go of her as he became aware of Britt standing quietly by the door. The smile faded from Bobby's face and was replaced with a look of curiosity.

She followed his glance. "Britt, this is my brother, Bobby. Bobby, this is Britt Carlton, my next-door neighbor." The two men shook hands. "Britt is the one responsible for my being here." She turned her gaze toward Britt and flashed a warm smile, then returned her attention to Bobby. "Britt's a pilot. Tomorrow he picks up a new jet and flies it back to Seattle. Since he was going to be in Wichita, anyway, he offered me a lift."

Bobby grinned at Britt. "Well, I certainly appreciate your generosity. This is a great graduation present."

"It was my pleasure." Britt turned his gaze on Ashley and shot her a quick wink. "I'm glad I was able to do it."

"Well, if you two will excuse me, I'll go out and say hello to Mom and Dad." Bobby hurried to the patio, leaving Britt and Ashley alone.

Britt clasped her hand in his. "I need to check with the Cessna sales office and also flight operations. I'll probably have to go there this afternoon to take care of some paperwork and officially assume delivery. Do you mind if I use the phone?" He drew her hand to his lips, kissing her palm while waiting for her answer.

"Of course you may use the phone. If you need to go there, let me know. I'll drive you." She felt a tingling sensation slowly spread from the spot where his lips touched her palm throughout her body.

"I'll be right back." He went to the other room to make his call.

She wandered out to the patio. Her mother, father and brother stared at her from where they were seated around the table. She felt the heat rush to her cheeks. "Why is everyone looking at me?"

"Well, sis, Mom and Dad were just filling me in on you and Britt." Bobby's serious expression quickly changed to a teasing grin. "Would you like equal time to give me your side of the story?"

She glanced down at the ground, knowing her entire face had turned bright crimson. She took several deep breaths, then looked up again as she managed a shy smile. "Will you guys cut it out? And *please,* don't talk like that in front of Britt. I told you, when—make that *if*— there's anything to announce, you'll be the first to know."

A moment later Britt appeared at the back door. "I do have to take care of that paperwork. I shouldn't be gone too long."

"I need to go to the grocery store for Mother," Ashley said. "I can drop you off, then pick you up when you're through."

"A buddy of mine in flight operations goes on his meal break in an hour and a half. He can give me a ride back when I'm through." He looked at her for a long minute, his face soft and loving. "Besides, you're here to see your family, not chauffeur me around town."

"I'm going to the grocery store now. Are you ready to go? I'll get my purse."

Ashley dropped Britt off at Cessna, then continued on to the grocery store. She checked the items on her mother's list and realized she would need a cart. She picked up some strawberries, a honeydew melon, three different types of cheese, some dip for the crackers and was headed toward the soft drinks when she heard someone call her name. She turned around and was jolted into stunned silence.

The handsome man with the dark curly hair smiled at her. "Hello, Ashley. It's good to see you again. Have you moved back to Wichita, or are you just visiting?"

It took her a moment before she found her voice. "Jerry...Jerry Broderick. What are you doing here?"

"Same as you I would imagine. I'm grocery shopping."

"Uh...yes, well...uh... I need to be going."

He reached out and grabbed hold of her cart to prevent her from hurrying down the aisle. "Please, Ashley...won't you give me just a few minutes of your time?"

She nervously glanced at her watch. "Well, maybe a

minute. I need to get back to my folks' house with these groceries. I'm just in town for the weekend for my brother's graduation party. I'm leaving again tomorrow.''

''I just want you to know how bad I feel about what happened.''

''Yes…well, that's nice. Now if you'll excuse—''

''Please hear me out. I sincerely feel rotten about what I did to you. I am so sorry for the pain I caused you. I'd still marry you in a heartbeat if you'd have me, but I know it's probably too late. I'm sure that bridge is burned.'' He hesitated a minute as he looked at her expectantly, a glimmer of hopefulness in his expression. ''Or is it? Do you think there's a chance that we could start again?''

She looked at the open honesty in his face. She believed him, believed that he was truly sorry about what had happened, but that did not change anything. ''No, Jerry. I gave you my trust and my love and you betrayed it. Whatever we may have had is over, and it can't be brought back.''

''I've done a lot of soul-searching since you left. I wish it were different, Ashley, but I do understand why you made the decision you did. I guess I can't blame you. One thing, though—if there's ever anything you need, you will let me know, won't you? I mean, if you're ever in trouble or anything like that. Okay?''

They continued to talk for a few minutes, the feel of their conversation turning from awkward to something more akin to a couple of friends who had not seen each other for a while.

After they parted company, she rushed to finish her shopping then hurried home. She decided there was no point in mentioning her accidental meeting with Jerry Broderick to Britt. Jerry was a part of her life before she met Britt and had nothing to do with it now. For her, seeing him had offered a sense of closure to a painful episode in her life. And she was happy to realize just how certain she was that she'd made the right decision. Seeing Jerry had been no different from running into an old college chum while home for a visit.

By six o'clock that evening the party was in full swing, an interesting assortment of people mingling and mixing—relatives, family friends and some of Bobby's college friends. Ashley noticed how easily Britt fit in with everyone, talking comfortably with strangers as if they were lifelong friends. More important to her was that her family seemed to genuinely like him—even the not-easily impressed Bobby was very taken with Britt.

She sat on the couch and watched as Britt mingled with the guests, sipped his club soda and, in short, charmed the pants off everyone. A golden glow, a warmth, generated from within and enveloped her. Every time he scanned the room searching for her, she felt a tremor of excitement in her stomach. When his gaze settled on her, he would smile warmly and wink. She reveled in the sensation of the way his eyes possessed her as if he were holding her in his arms.

By ten o'clock the last of the guests had extended their goodbyes and departed. Ashley stifled a yawn; she had not gotten as much sleep the night before as she should have—not that she regretted even one second of the cause. A smile turned the corners of her mouth, and a warm feeling permeated every part of her as she thought of the promise she and Britt had made to each other—the promise of the right time and the right place.

Britt caught a glimpse of her smile as Ashley nestled into the corner of the couch. She looked so delicious. It was all he could do to keep from gobbling her up. He wanted to hold her, run his fingers through her silky hair, feel the creamy smoothness of her skin, taste the sweetness of her mouth. An inaudible sigh escaped his lips as he resigned himself to the situation—one more night in her parents' home before they returned to Seattle. He tried to stifle a yawn, but was not successful.

Marilyn caught his attempt to cover his yawn. "Oh, dear, Britt. We're keeping you up, aren't we? Here we kept you up until three o'clock this morning, and now we're headed for another late night. I imagine you need your sleep if you're going to be flying that jet back to Seattle in the morning." Marilyn rose from the couch, walked over to Britt and patted him on the hand as she gave him a warm, motherly smile. "Now don't you stay up just to be polite. If you're tired, you feel free to go to bed."

"That's right, Britt," Mike added. "We don't stand on ceremony in this house."

"Perhaps I will turn in. Ashley and I have an earlier takeoff than originally scheduled. We'll be leaving at nine o'clock in the morning. I'll need to be at Cessna's airfield by eight o'clock for the preflight check."

Ashley looked at him questioningly. "Why so early? Is there a problem?"

"That's the departure time Cessna gave me." It was only a little lie, but his newly formed plans hinged on them getting back to Seattle by early afternoon rather than later in the evening...plans he had initiated with the phone call he had made while taking care of the paperwork for the plane.

Bobby had been listening intently to the exchange. He jumped into the conversation. "Britt, why don't I take you in the morning for your preflight check? Maybe you could take a few minutes to show me the plane? I've never been in a private jet before. I thought they needed two pilots. Is someone else flying back with you?"

"Most business jets require a pilot and copilot. This particular model only needs one pilot."

Bobby shot a quick look at his parents, then returned his attention to Britt. "Mom and Dad can bring Ashley out later. Is that okay with everyone?"

Britt rose from his chair. "It's okay with me. Do you mind?" he addressed his question to Mike and Marilyn.

Mike responded immediately. "Not at all."

"Then it's settled. I'll see everyone in the morning. Good night." Britt's smile lingered on Ashley.

She returned his look. "Good night." Her gaze followed his retreating form as he disappeared down the darkened hallway.

It was after eleven o'clock when Ashley climbed into bed and pulled the lightweight cover up to her waist. She had just switched off the lamp on the nightstand and closed her eyes when she heard a faint tapping at the bathroom door. She slipped out of bed, padded barefoot across the carpeted floor and opened the door. Britt grabbed her wrist and pulled her to him.

"I couldn't go to sleep without saying good-night to you properly, or at least as proper as possible for here and now." He quickly captured her mouth as she wrapped her arms around him, embracing his energy.

His lips burned hot against hers; his passion flowed into her. He darted his tongue between her lips. There were moments when she actually felt light-headed, as if she could not get enough oxygen. He literally took her breath away.

His hands stroked the length of her torso, the gentleness of his touch in sharp contrast to the urgency of his kiss and the fiery thrust of his tongue. Each upward stroke of his hand pulled her soft T-shirt farther up her body until it was bunched up just above her hips. His hand slipped under the soft fabric as he stroked her smooth skin. His fingers played across the roundness of her bottom, tenderly caressed her bare back and moved along her rib cage to the petite roundness of her breasts.

The gentle stroking of his fingers sent tremors across her bare skin. Her legs felt weak. The very air around them sizzled with sexual electricity. His hand closed over her breast, then a soft moan escaped her throat. Instinctively she arched her back, forcing herself more fully into his hand, her puckered nipple tight against his palm.

She felt his hardness press against her stomach, the fabric of his briefs barely containing his arousal. Her hands wandered over the taut muscle tone of his well-built body—his broad shoulders, his hard chest, his strong back and arms.

With great difficulty Britt drew his head back from her, his breathing labored and ragged—as was hers. Her body seemed to be shaking as much as his with uncontrolled tremors. "If we don't stop doing this immediately...I swear, I'm going to take you right here on the bathroom floor—right now." The husky tone made his voice barely recognizable, even to himself. He placed his fingers under her chin, lifted her face to his and softly brushed her lips. "I can't take much more of this. You excite me so much, I nearly lose all control of my sense and reason."

She looked into the smoldering charcoal depths of his eyes and spoke in a quavering voice barely above a whisper. "I can't take much more of this, either." Slowly she turned toward her bedroom as she said, "Good night, Britt."

He watched as she disappeared into her room, closing the door behind her. The sensation of their lips pressed together lingered with him for several moments. A very real emotional jolt also clung to him, feelings that went beyond the mere physical. He had not planned on it happening and he was not even sure exactly when it did happen, but like it or not he was emotionally involved. In a barely audible whisper he said, "Good night, my love."

Britt woke at six-thirty the next morning. He wanted to stay in bed, but he knew there was no way. He had to shower, pack, extend his thanks to Marilyn and Mike and be at the airfield by eight o'clock.

Ashley finally emerged from her bedroom at a few minutes after eight. "Good morning, Daddy." She gave him a quick hug then continued on to the kitchen. "Good morning, Mother." She poured herself a cup of coffee as she looked around. "Where is everyone?"

Marilyn smiled at her daughter. "If by *everyone* you mean Britt, you just missed him. He and Bobby left a couple of minutes ago."

The disappointment clearly showed on Ashley's face.

"Don't be so glum, dear. You'll be seeing him in—"

The ringing phone interrupted Marilyn's sentence. Her face took on a very stern look as she listened to the caller. Her voice was cold, her words clipped, as she answered. "I'll see if she wants to talk to you." She placed her hand over the receiver to muffle her words and turned toward Ashley. "It's Jerry Broderick. Do you want to talk to him? I can tell him you already left."

"It's okay, Mother. I'll talk to him. I ran into Jerry at the grocery store yesterday and we had a nice conversation. He said he'd be calling to say goodbye before I left today."

Britt touched the jet down in Seattle for a perfect landing. Forty-five minutes later he and Ashley were at her front door. After she stepped inside her apartment, he leaned forward and kissed her lightly on the lips.

He looked at his watch. "It's only one-thirty. Why don't we have an early dinner, say about five o'clock?" He leaned forward and kissed her again. He started to pull away but lingered as his fingertips danced lightly across her cheek. "Mmm...you're difficult to get away from, but I've got to go. I have an errand to run. I'll see you later."

A bit of a frown wrinkled her brow as she closed the door. She took her time unpacking, then poured herself a glass of iced tea. She plopped down on the couch and tried to get interested in a magazine. She glanced at the clock. It had been an hour and she had not seen or heard any evidence of his having returned. She vacillated between confusion and concern. She was not sure exactly what she'd expected to happen when they got home, but this certainly was not it. It was almost as if he could not get away from her fast enough. She replayed the events of the previous two days through her mind as she continued to keep an eye on the balcony door. Surely he would appear any minute. Or was it possible that he wasn't as anxious about the evening as she was?

The sharp buzz of the doorbell intruded into her thoughts. She went to see who it was.

"Miss Ashley Thornton?"

"Yes, I'm Ashley Thornton."

"Delivery. Please sign here."

She signed the receipt, and the man handed her a long box from a local florist.

"Just a minute, let me get my purse."

"No need. The tip has been taken care of. Have a nice day."

She carried the box to her dining table, slipped off the ribbon and removed the lid. The box contained two dozen

long-stemmed roses and a card. Her fingers trembled as
she removed the card from its envelope and read the message. *Brittlow Pennington Carlton requests the pleasure
of Ashley Marie Thornton's company for dinner at his
residence. Champagne at four o'clock, dinner at five
o'clock.*

Her eyes filled with tears as an overwhelming feeling
of joy soared inside her. She held the card to her heart as
she gazed at the beautiful roses. She fought back her tears
as she took a crystal vase from the top shelf of a cupboard.
After carefully arranging the flowers, she set the vase in
the living room next to the couch. She picked up the card
and read it again, shaking her head in disbelief. She carried the card with her as she went to the dressing room
to select what she would wear.

At precisely four o'clock Ashley rang Britt's doorbell.
The door opened and he stood before her in a black tux,
white pleated shirt and cummerbund. He looked so handsome, so very elegant. He held his hand out to assist her
through the door. She was so choked with emotion that
she was barely able to speak. "Thank you for the roses.
They're lovely."

"It was my pleasure." He could not take his eyes off
her. She looked beautiful, more beautiful than anything
he had ever seen. She seemed to glow, to emit an opal-
escent aura that totally enveloped her.

She wore a simple white strapless dress with fitted bodice and straight skirt. A turquoise sash stretched over her
right shoulder; the other shoulder was bare. She wore no
jewelry. Her hair hung loose, falling almost to her shoulders, and feathered softly around her face. She smelled of
tea roses—a light scent, yet one that was instantly addic-
tive as the sensual fragrance wafted past his nostrils. She
held one of the roses in her hand.

He felt the warmth of her touch as she accepted the offer of his hand. A tremor moved through his body. He continued to hold her hand as he escorted her into the dimly lit living room. The dining table had been set for a formal meal—china, crystal, silver, a small floral centerpiece with white tapers. He led her to the couch and stepped aside as she sat down.

She felt as if she were part of a dream, an ethereal experience that happened only once in a lifetime. When she had taken his hand, shivers of delight swept through her. His touch was warm, gentle and loving. "I'm overwhelmed, Britt. I don't know what to say."

He looked adoringly at her. "You're very beautiful," he said, his voice soft, his halting words conveying the strong emotions that coursed through him. He kissed the palm of her hand and held it briefly against his cheek before releasing it. "I'll pour some champagne."

He lifted his glass as he seated himself next to her on the couch. "I'd like to propose a toast." She raised her glass to his. "Here's to a special evening with a very special lady who has become very important to my life."

They clinked glasses as she looked into his darkening silver eyes. She felt the rush of heat to her cheeks as she lowered her lashes, her embarrassment preventing her from holding his look. "Thank you." Her voice was almost a whisper.

Various emotions collided within her as she sipped from her glass. She knew if all the emotions were fused into a single entity, it would be the one thing she had wanted most to avoid—her very personal and very real feelings for Britt Carlton. She was afraid to even think of the word *love*. She knew she was in way over her head, but she did not know how to get out. For her, their relationship had moved way beyond the state of just friends.

Was she making another mistake? Was she doomed to repeat her previous error in judgment where men were concerned? She was so certain about what she wanted, yet so afraid of what it meant.

When they finished their champagne, he stood and offered her his arm. "I believe our table is ready."

After they finished dinner, he took her hand and led her from the dining room to the living room and poured each of them a brandy. They sipped from their glasses, each totally enveloped in the blanket of emotion that surrounded them.

When she took the last sip from her glass, he reached out and took it from her hand. "Would you like something else?"

She leaned over and lightly brushed her lips against his. An impish grin tugged at her mouth. "That's a leading question if ever I heard one."

"Oh?" He answered her implied challenge with a mischievous grin of his own. "And just what is it you have in mind?"

Their gazes locked in a heated moment that elevated their passion to an unknown plane of excitement. The air sizzled. They found themselves being drawn down a path from which there would be no turning back. The line between friends and lovers was about to be erased. Could the two extremes be combined into one, or would making love be the ruination of their friendship? It was a possibility that neither of them could deny, but each chose to ignore.

Ashley rested her hand against his chest. "Dinner was delicious. This evening has been enchanting. You're wonderful."

He put his arm around her shoulder and pulled her close to his side. He spoke softly, reflectively. "No, I'm not wonderful. I'm just a man in—'' The words caught in his throat. To tell her he loved her implied a commitment, something he could not give her. The words refused to leave his mouth.

He lifted her chin with his fingertips and looked into her eyes for a long moment before lowering his head, his mouth savoring the tiny droplets of brandy that clung to her soft lips. ''You taste delicious, but I'm not quite sure what flavor that is. May I have another sample?''

Her insides trembled as she spoke. ''I think you should just keep sampling until you figure it out.''

His voice was low and husky. ''I think you're right.'' Again, he lowered his head and captured her mouth. He nibbled softly at the corners and then at her lower lip before allowing his tongue to seek out hers. The distinctive taste of the brandy filled his mouth, combined with her own natural sweetness.

He felt himself racing out of control. He wanted it all. He wanted to know every inch of her; he wanted her to know every inch of him. He wanted to make love to her, totally and completely. His lips smothered her with a frenzy of kisses—her neck, her throat, her face. Then his mouth hungrily devoured hers as his hands moved over the smooth fabric of her dress, up the fitted bodice to her breasts.

Her breathing quickened; sensual stirrings took control of her body. Her entire reality at that moment centered on how much she wanted Britt to make love to her. The evening had been perfect; now was truly the right time and the right place.

Her hands moved frantically inside his tux jacket, her fingers fumbling with the shirt studs, trying to get at his bare skin. She hungered for him as much as he obviously wanted her.

"Ashley..." he murmured in her ear, his voice thick with the passion that stirred inside him. His mouth moved down her throat as she threw her head back, arching her neck toward him. "Come to bed with me...now." He stood up, taking her hands in his.

She stood beside him, her entire body on fire. Her breath came in quick gasps as she spoke. "Yes, oh yes...please, Britt, right now."

He quickly removed his jacket and dropped it to the floor as she stepped out of her high heels. He scooped her up in his arms and carried her toward his bedroom. She untied his tie and removed some of his shirt studs. Having finally exposed part of his bare chest, she leaned her head down and provocatively ran the tip of her tongue across the exposed skin.

He moaned, the sound both hungry and urgent. "Be careful. If you surprise me like that again, I might end up dropping you."

She tickled her tongue across his bare skin again. "If you do drop me, try to drop me on the bed."

He placed her on the floor so she stood next to his bed. His eyes gleamed a dark smoldering charcoal. "I have a feeling I'll be lucky to come out of this alive, but I can't think of any way I'd rather go." His words came out in ragged gasps.

She tugged his shirttail out of the waistband of his trousers, quickly removed the remaining shirt studs, then ran her hands across his bare chest. She splayed her fingers in order to touch as much of him as possible. A low moan escaped his lips as her touch moved across his skin.

He reached his arms around her, his fingers searching for the zipper at the back of her dress. He pulled the tab down, then watched as she slipped out of the dress, his gaze riveted to the silky fabric that dropped past her bare breasts, past her slim hips and pooled at her feet. She wore only panty hose and a pair of white lace bikini panties.

"Oh, Ashley…" He moved his hands to her breasts, her dusky nipples already hardened to taut buds. "So delicate…"

"They're much too small."

"No, they're not." He kicked off his shoes as he sat on the edge of the bed and pulled her to him. Gently he cupped one breast with his hand. "So perfect…so delicate and pink…so exquisite." He bent his head toward her other breast, taking only her taut nipple between his lips. He held it in the moist warmth of his mouth for a few seconds as the tip of his tongue played across the enticing texture before taking in more of her soft succulent flesh.

She sighed deeply as her eyes closed and a smile curled her lips. She wrapped her arms around his neck, ran her fingers through his thick sandy hair, then placed one hand at the back of his head. A shudder shot through her body as he drew more of her flesh into his mouth and gently suckled. Her mind whirled in a sensual fog. Every place he touched her sent tingling sensations across her skin and caused her insides to tremble. She wanted more and more of him.

He released her nipple from his mouth as he rose shakily to his feet, taking her face in his trembling hands. "I knew you'd taste like that—so sweet, so delicate…" He quickly captured her mouth as his hands caressed her bare back. His fingers danced across the texture of her skin.

She returned his passion, their tongues dancing together. His kisses were maddening. She had not known it was possible to be driven to such excitement by mere kisses. She moved her hands slowly down his bare chest. When she reached the cummerbund, her arms slipped around his waist and her fingers fumbled, but she could not seem to unfasten it. Her irritation at the barrier grew as she pulled at it. "How do you get this thing off?" Her breathless words conveyed a sense of urgency and irritation.

He took her hands in his and kissed her fingertips. "I'll do that, if you'll grapple with those panty hose of yours." His voice was thick and low as he forced out the words.

A minute later they stood together next to the bed, their clothes scattered on the floor, their nude bodies not quite touching. Each trembled with the excitement of sweet anticipation, enthralled by the events unfolding before them. Tenderly he wrapped his arms around her, drawing her to him, resting his cheek against the top of her head.

She encircled his waist with her arms as she placed her head against his chest. She could hear his strong heartbeat, feel the rise and fall of his chest with each breath he took. She had never felt like this before and did not want the feeling to ever end.

The frantic turmoil that had possessed them just a short time earlier had been replaced by the calming knowledge that the night was still very young. They had several hours in which to savor all the delights of lovemaking—intimate foreplay, the joining of their bodies and finally the warm afterglow of their union.

Britt scooped her up in his arms then bent his head to kiss the tempting valley nestled between her breasts. He heard her sigh as his tongue teased her nipples. He placed her gently in the middle of his bed, stretched his tall frame next to her, ran his fingers through her long dark hair, then lightly caressed her cheek with his fingertips. He planted little kisses on the side of her neck, then whispered softly in her ear, "I want this night to be special for you, very special."

His soft words sent shivers down her spine. "You've

already made this night very special." She slowly rubbed her bare leg against his, the sensations causing her body to tingle. She had never felt so alive, so filled with the joy of simply being.

He recaptured her mouth. Their breathing became ragged as their passion began building again. His hands caressed the curves of her body. His fingers stroked the smooth skin on her shoulders, trailed across her stomach, outlined her hip. He nuzzled her neck as he cupped her breast, her nipple still puckered and taut. His tongue trailed from the notch at the base of her throat to the skin between her breasts.

He rolled over and pulled her body on top of his. A tingle of excitement added to his already aroused state. His mouth captured hers in a kiss that said more than he wanted it to, but he could not stop his inner feelings from showing.

She was everything he needed...everything he wanted. Her body seemed to mold to his, her heated excitement rivaling his own. He had to touch her everywhere, know all of her. With their bodies wrapped together, they rolled over until his torso partially covered hers. His fingers tickled up her inner thigh until they reached the moist heat of her femininity. He broke away from her mouth, but only long enough to seek out her puckered nipple.

Ashley's ragged breathing matched his with each breath she drew. The thrill of his touch surged through her body. Her arms tightened around him and an audible moan of pleasure escaped her throat when his mouth closed over her hardened nipple. Making love had never felt as right as it did with Britt Carlton.

She felt his back muscles flex beneath her hands. A quick shiver of anticipation jolted through her when his fingers grazed the downy softness at the apex of her thighs, then slipped inside her. The sensations spread out until they heated every corner of her existence, building until the level of excitement reached the ultimate pinnacle. She thrust her body hard against his hand and held him tightly within her embrace.

He recaptured her mouth with a demanding intensity, the provocative allure of her taste being almost more than he could handle. He felt her body convulse, then felt the soft moan that whispered across his ear. He raised himself up on one elbow and attempted to bring his labored breathing under control. He smoothed her hair back from her face. Her eyes glowed with an inner fire. Her slightly parted lips emphasized the lush fullness of her mouth. He brushed a soft kiss across her cheek, then cupped her breast in his hand. He placed an equally soft kiss on each nipple.

Britt reached a slightly shaky hand toward the night-stand, pulled open the drawer and removed a packet. He ripped it open and removed the contents. A moment later he snuggled his body between her thighs.

Ashley felt his heat settle over her as he covered her body with his. Her heart pounded a hard rhythm, one that matched the strong beat that reverberated from his chest to hers. The intensity of his passion never wavered, with her own desires matching his in every sensual touch and stroke.

He thrust forward, filling her with his hardness. She held him tightly as she arched her hips to meet his. They remained still while savoring the first intimate joining of their bodies, then he set a slow pace that gradually esca-lated, each moving in rhythmic harmony with the other.

Ashley experienced wondrous sensations of euphoria with Britt. She soared to the heights, rode the crest of a tidal wave, and finally succumbed to the delicious rapture that totally claimed her. The convulsions started deep inside her and quickly enveloped her entire body. She clung tightly to Britt, the powerful waves of ecstasy that crashed through her almost overwhelming her ability to think.

Britt strained against the limits of his control. His chest heaved as he tried to suck in more air. He gave one last deep thrust, then shuddered as the spasms rippled through him. He remained deep inside her as he wrapped her tightly in his embrace. He buried his face in her hair to prevent the words from escaping his mouth—the words that would have revealed his innermost feelings. They were words he was not prepared to say, feelings he might never be able to share with her.

He finally lifted his face from where it nestled at the juncture of her neck and shoulder. He slowly focused his gaze on her. A moment later he was startled into reality by the sight of her tear-filled eyes.

"Ashley?" His voice carried the anxiety he could not hide. He wiped the tears from her cheeks with his fingers and tenderly kissed each eyelid. He held her tightly as he spoke softly into her ear, his voice conveying his concern. "I didn't hurt you, did I? Please tell me I didn't. I'm so sorry. Are you okay? What can I do?"

9

Ashley smiled at him through the mist of her tears. "I'm fine, honest." She kissed him softly, seductively, drawing his lower lip into her mouth and holding it there for a moment before laying her head back on the pillow. "In fact, I've never been better in my entire life. Oh, Britt...that was so...so..." The tears started to stream down her cheeks again as her face displayed the total spectrum of joyful emotions that engulfed her.

They silently held each other, lost in their own world. Britt continued to stroke her hair, to cherish their oneness. He became aware of the slow, steady rhythm of her breathing. He glanced down at her face and saw that her eyes were closed. He closed his eyes, the silkiness of her skin thrilling his senses as his fingertips caressed her back and shoulders. He was soon asleep, too.

Sometime later Ashley woke, slowly becoming aware that she was alone in Britt's bed. She squinted at the clock on the nightstand, the red numerals glowing in the darkened room. It was only eleven o'clock. It seemed as though it should be much later; she felt as if she had been sleeping for a long time, not just two hours. She glanced toward his bathroom. The door was ajar and the room dark.

She slipped out of bed and picked up his tux shirt from

the floor. She put it on, wrapping it around her like a robe. It smelled of his aftershave, the scent causing her to shiver slightly as it called forth the memory of the many delicious sensations shared earlier that evening.

The light coming from the kitchen drew her attention as she padded silently through the darkened apartment. She paused at the kitchen door for a moment. A loving feeling, touched with a hint of amusement, filled her with a warm glow as she watched him.

Britt stood across from the refrigerator, leaning back against the countertop. He had not bothered to put on any clothes, not even a robe. He held a spoon in one hand, a carton of ice cream in the other. As if suddenly sensing her presence, he jerked his head around and locked gazes with her. His embarrassment forced him to shove the carton back in the freezer.

He sheepishly recaptured her look as he started across the room in her direction. "It looks like you caught me. I admit it, I'm an ice cream junkie." He placed a tender kiss on her lips, put his arm around her shoulder, then they returned to the bedroom.

An hour later all was quiet except for the sound of her breathing as she slept peacefully in his arms. Her long lashes rested delicately against her upper cheek, while her hand lay against his hard chest, her head on his shoulder. Her breasts rose and fell with the even rhythm of her breathing, as he played with the feathery tresses of her glossy hair.

He knew he had become emotionally involved with her, but he had not been prepared for the profound impact their lovemaking had on him. He loved her. That knowledge scared him to death, but he knew it was true. What he did not know was what to do about it. He kissed her softly on the forehead, then closed his eyes and finally fell asleep.

"Britt, wake up." Ashley shook his shoulder. "It's six-thirty. I have to be at work by eight o'clock." She edged toward the side of the bed as he slowly opened his eyes.

"Tell Stu you found something better to do today." His voice was thick with sleep. "Tell him you decided to spend the day letting me ravish your body." He reached over and grabbed her hand as she slid out from under the covers, pulling her down on top of him. "You know..." He seductively trailed his fingertips down her back and across the perfect curve of her bare bottom. "I never did kiss that frostbite and make it better. How's it doing?"

A teasing chuckle escaped her throat. "Are you sure you didn't? If not, then it's the only place you missed." Her voice softened as she snuggled back against the warmth of his body. "Thank you for last night. The roses were beautiful, the champagne and candlelight were enchanting, the dinner was delicious, and afterward..."

He lifted her face and gazed into her eyes as he spoke in almost a whisper. "It all pales into nothingness when compared to what you gave me."

Before Ashley knew it, half the workday was over, and she was hungry. There had not been time to grab any breakfast. She had just barely made it to work by eight o'clock as it was. She looked forward to a quiet hour where she could sit and reflect on the happenings of the previous weekend. Closing her eyes, she leaned back in her chair as her mind drifted to tantalizing thoughts of Britt Carlton.

"Excuse me, Ashley." Stu Billington's voice startled her out of her moment of reverie.

"I'm sorry, Stu. I'm afraid I was doing a little day-dreaming."

Stu gave her a warm smile. "Big event of some sort coming up?"

She looked down at her desk, then up at Stu. She could not stop the shy look of embarrassment she knew had quickly darted across her face or the rush of heat she felt on her cheeks. "No, the big event was just this past week-end." She offered no further explanation, and Stu did not ask.

Ashley was very busy for the balance of the workday. When five o'clock finally arrived, she cleared off the top of her desk and left her office. As soon as she arrived home, she changed clothes and turned on the TV to catch the evening news. Before curling up in the corner of the couch, she paused a moment to inhale the fragrance of the roses Britt had given her. She had just settled into the couch, tucking her legs under her, when she heard Britt at her balcony door. She rushed to let him in, her heart pounding with excitement.

He stepped into her apartment and immediately wrapped his arms around her, drawing her against his body, holding her tightly as he rested his cheek against the top of her head. She melted into his embrace, reveling in the warmth of his touch.

His soft voice whispered in her ear. "I'm glad you're home. I missed you."

His words were like music—soft and soothing while at the same time exciting. She fell under his spell, losing her grip on rational thinking. She tried to regain control of her emotions. In a faltering voice she asked, "Would you like something to eat? I could fix us some dinner."

"Maybe later." He attempted to cover the depth of his feelings for her with a teasing manner. "For now, I'll just nibble on this—'' He seductively nipped at the corners of her mouth with his lips. ''And this—'' He drew her lower lip into his mouth. Time and place became a blur as their clothes tumbled to the floor and they sank into a oneness of body and soul. Their lovemaking proved to be every bit as intense as it had been the night before and with it the emotional stakes grew even higher.

Much later Ashley teased him as she cleared the last of the dinner dishes from the table. ''I'm sorry I don't have any ice cream, especially now that I know your secret vice.''

Britt followed her from the table, watching her closely as she placed the dishes in the dishwasher and added the soap. He slipped his arms around her waist and turned her to him. ''I enjoyed a fantastic dessert before we had dinner.''

She felt the color rise in her cheeks as the full meaning of his soft words floated over her. She leaned against his hard body, resting her head on his chest as he reached his hand up to stroke her hair. ''Oh, Britt…you make me feel so special.''

He held her gently against his body, pressed his cheek against her hair and answered softly, ''You are so special.'' They stood together, savoring the quietness of the moment.

Slowly he released her from his arms and looked into her eyes. ''I'd better go home. I have an early flight tomorrow morning. I need to get some sleep, and I'm sure not going to be able to do that if I stay here.'' He kissed her tenderly on the lips, then gave her one last lingering look before leaving.

The next day was a busy one for Ashley. She and Stu worked frantically to pull together all the loose ends of an important project, prior to a meeting that Stu had scheduled.

"I think we're going to have to redo these reports. I just finished talking to Ed Simpson, and the information he provided me allows us to expand in these two areas." Stu placed the folder on her desk, indicating two specific reports. "I've outlined what I need, so if you could take care of these for me—"

She looked questioningly at him. "Did you want these done tonight?"

"No, I don't need them before noon Friday." Stu looked at his watch. "Well, no wonder you were asking. It's almost seven o'clock. You should have been out of here two hours ago." He headed back to his office. "Good night, Ashley. I'll see you in the morning."

"Good night, Stu."

Ashley went straight home. It had been a long day, and she was exhausted. She switched on the table lamp next to the couch, then went to the kitchen to grab a quick bite to eat. She heard a tapping at her balcony, and her spirit brightened as she hurried to open the door.

"Hi." His voice was soft and loving as he immediately swept her into his arms and held her close.

"Hi, yourself." She stifled a yawn.

A teasing grin tugged at the corners of Britt's mouth. "I was afraid this day would arrive. You've become bored with me." Even though he tried to make his words sound as if he were teasing, he could not stop the thought that it might be true—a portent of things to come. He forced the errant thoughts out of his mind. "However, I would think good manners would dictate that you at least wait until I leave before you start yawning." He kissed the tip of her nose, then rested his cheek against her head. "Did you have a rough day?'' His tone was caring as he lightly stroked her hair.

She closed her eyes as a contented sigh escaped her lips. ''No, it wasn't that rough, but it was long. I just now got home from work.''

He led her over to the couch. ''Here, why don't you kick off your shoes and relax. I'll fix you something to eat.''

''That sounds great.'' She gave him a grateful smile. ''I could sure get used to being waited on like this.'' She sank into the couch, leaned back against the pillows and closed her eyes.

Britt went to her kitchen and a little while later stuck his head out the door and called to her. ''Soup's on.'' When she did not respond, he went to the living room and found her sleeping on the couch. He knelt on the floor next to her, leaned forward and kissed her tenderly on the forehead before leaving her to get some much-needed sleep.

Ashley didn't know when Britt had left her apartment. She awoke the next morning just in time to get ready for work. She was busy at her desk when the phone interrupted her. The sound of Britt's voice sent little shivers over the surface of her skin.

''I just got a call on a flight. We leave in two hours. I'll be in Denver, Kansas City, Chicago and St. Louis. I'll be home Friday afternoon.'' He paused as a sudden thought struck him. ''Your birthday is this weekend. Do you have any plans, starting early Saturday morning and carrying on until late Sunday night?''

''Except for the routine stuff like cleaning, laundry and grocery shopping—nothing important. Why?''

"Good! Don't make any plans. I'll see you Friday evening. I should be home before you are."

"Would you like to tell me what you have planned just in case I might have some objections?" Her voice was warm as she kidded with him about his proprietary attitude.

He feigned hurt feelings. "How could you possibly have any objections to my plans?"

During the next few days Ashley kept herself busy, trying not to notice how slowly time passed. She hurried home from work Friday evening, looking forward to their evening together. She freshened up and changed her clothes, selecting a pair of silk slacks with matching silk blouse. She sprayed herself with just a hint of her favorite perfume.

Britt had been home for about an hour. He unpacked his bag and changed clothes. He was anxious to see Ashley, since it had been several days since they had been together. He contorted his features into a confused scowl. It was very disturbing to him, the way he so totally wanted her. But what was even more disconcerting was that he *needed* her. He had never really needed anyone before. It was as if he wasn't whole without her. The realization totally overwhelmed him—and scared him to death.

He left his apartment and hopped over to her balcony. Moments later a rush of excitement bolted through him as his arms surrounded her and his lips touched hers. The tenderness of the moment, the joy of simply being with her, surpassed the urgency of the passion that had been churning inside him.

It also shoved his concerns into the background, concerns about his feelings for her and what to do about them. He held her closely and nuzzled the side of her neck.

His voice was soft and loving as he whispered in her ear, "Come away with me for the weekend."

"Where do you want to go?"

"Does it matter?"

"No, it doesn't matter at all." Her mouth found his, as once again they were enveloped in a warm cocoon.

"Come on, hurry. We'll be late." Britt stood at Ashley's front door, holding their overnight bags. She had gone back to her closet to grab a lightweight jacket.

"I don't suppose you're going to tell me where we're going. You know, that makes it very difficult to pack." She appeared from the hallway, carrying her jacket. "I guess I'm ready."

A blatantly lascivious glint radiated from the silvery depths of his eyes. "If you're at a loss about what to pack, then don't pack anything. We could spend the entire weekend in our room."

She returned his look as she seductively purred in his ear, "We don't need to leave town for that."

He held her look as he bit at his lower lip. "Don't tempt me like that." He grabbed her hand. "Come on or we'll miss the boat."

"The boat? We're going somewhere on a boat?"

He grinned mischievously. "Didn't I mention that part? I hope you don't get seasick."

An hour later they boarded a high-speed passenger ferry running between the Seattle waterfront and the city of Victoria on Vancouver Island in British Columbia. Ashley was seated next to one of the large picture windows, enjoying the scenery, when Britt appeared, carrying two cups of coffee. "Here." He handed one of the cups to her. "Watch it, it's very hot."

She took the cup from his hand. "Thanks." Her enthusiasm bubbled over as she spoke. "This is so exciting. I've never been in a boat on the ocean." She shot him an impish grin. "I hope it's slightly less nerve-racking than being in a small airplane on the ocean."

He returned her grin. "You're never going to let me live that down, are you?"

Her excitement grew as the catamaran moved sleekly through the water of Elliott Bay and out into Puget Sound. The Seattle skyline faded from view as they headed north toward Canada, finally arriving at the inner harbor of Victoria. They claimed their luggage and quickly cleared customs.

Her face radiated her excitement as she looked around the streets and across the harbor. Each streetlight contained a basket of brightly colored flowers that hung below the lamp globes. Red British double-decker buses were parked in front of the landmark Empress Hotel. Britt watched her as she took in each new sight. It was the same type of enthusiasm she had exhibited when he'd taken her sight-seeing in Seattle. "Come on, let's check in at the hotel and then do some sight-seeing."

After checking in and unpacking, they left the hotel to explore the city. Following a full afternoon, they dined in an intimate little restaurant overlooking the harbor. They savored the meal, oblivious to everything and everyone except each other. Slowly they walked hand in hand back to the hotel and to their room.

Britt went immediately to the dresser and opened a drawer, extracting a long velvet box. He handed it to her. "Happy Birthday."

Ashley took the box from him, her eyes wide with surprise. It was obviously a box from a jewelry store. Her fingers trembled slightly as she opened the card.

Dearest Ashley: May the joy of this day carry you

through the year. Thank you for allowing me to share it with you. Happy Birthday. Always, Britt.

She read the card twice as shifting emotions welled inside her. He had signed the card *Always* but not *Love.*

He caught the brief look of disappointment that darted across her face. "Ashley?" He stepped closer to her, taking a moment to caress her cheek. "Is something wrong?" A hint of trepidation shivered across his skin, a foreboding he could not quite place. He tried to shake it away, but it refused to completely disappear.

She smiled at him as she reached out to return his caress. "Nothing's wrong. I'm just so overwhelmed." She opened the box. Her eyes glowed with delight as her gaze lit on the gold bracelet.

"Oh, Britt. It's gorgeous." She immediately fastened it around her wrist. "Thank you for the beautiful bracelet. It's lovely." She leaned forward and kissed him lightly on the lips. "And thank you for this weekend."

"Thank you for sharing it with me." He knew in his heart and in his mind that no one would ever touch his soul the way she did.

Ashley had not meant for him to notice her disappointment over the way he had signed the card. She immediately tried to smooth it over by putting as much enthusiasm into her voice as she could. "We can do this again, can't we? I mean, go away for the weekend like this? This is so exciting. There are so many things we can do." She furrowed her brow for a second as she digested a sudden thought. "I don't expect you to always pay for everything. I can pay my share, too, now that I'm working again." She brightened again as she continued. "In fact, next time it will be my treat."

The feeling of foreboding welled inside him, returning even stronger than before. He tried to shove it back down.

His voice was soft as a caress, belying the sudden jolt of panic her words had caused. "For right now, why don't we just concentrate on tonight?" He had not been prepared for her sudden outburst that assumed they would always be doing things together. Even her offer to pay indicated she thought of them as a *couple* rather than two friends doing things together. Was she also assuming some sort of commitment?

The last thing he wanted was to lose her, but the entire commitment thing scared him. He had tried it before and it had led to disaster and four years of an empty life. Now that things were beginning to turn around, he didn't want to spoil them by tempting a repeat of history. Time.... He needed time to try to figure out what to do. He felt as if he were trapped between the proverbial rock and a hard place. No matter what he did, he feared it would be the wrong thing.

He had given a lot of thought to the card he had enclosed with the bracelet. He had wanted to sign the card "Love," but could not bring himself to do it. He wanted to say something personal, but not so personal that she would leap to any conclusions. Things were good between them just as they were. He feared what a change might bring. He also feared what his life would be like without her.

"That's a good idea." She wrapped her arms around his neck as he lifted her and carried her to the bed.

First thing the next morning they picked up the rental car that Britt had arranged. They packed, checked out of the hotel and started north out of Victoria. They soon arrived at Butchart Gardens. Ashley was immediately captivated by the beauty and serenity. She had never seen such an expanse of colorful flowers, landscaped gardens and fountains.

As Ashley stood next to him, poised at the top of the stairs leading down into the sunken garden, Britt studied her carefully. She seemed to be transported to another time or place, lost in her own private moment of reflection. He could not stop the slight frown that wrinkled his brow, a frown that coincided with the tremor of anxiety that started in the pit of his stomach again. He wondered where her thoughts were taking her. Was she really starting to pull away? How could he stop it?

For a brief moment he thought about Joan and how she had walked out on him for an old boyfriend. He didn't understand what had prompted the recollection, and he quickly shook the disturbing memory from his mind. But as soon as he dismissed that thought, another equally disturbing one immediately replaced it—a thought about Ashley and commitment and repeating past mistakes. He had been down that road before. He did allow that if he was ever going to be foolish enough to try it again, that Ashley would be the one.

He wrapped his arm around her shoulder and felt her jump when he startled her out of her private reverie. "I'm sorry, I didn't mean to scare you. You looked like you were a million miles away." He reached up and brushed a stray tendril of hair away from her cheek. "Anything you'd care to share?" Did he really want an honest answer to that question? He felt himself sinking further into despair.

She smiled as she leaned her head against his shoulder for a brief moment. "No, nothing. I was just lost in all of the beauty. When we walked up this path following the small sign that said Sunken Garden, I never dreamed all this—" she waved her arm across the horizon, taking in the entire expanse of the scene that spread out before her ''—was what I was going to see. This is breathtaking.''

She continued to stand at the head of the stairs, looking out across the beauty of the colorful gardens. A fleeting moment of disappointment darted through her body. She had tried to ignore it, pass it off as nothing, but the reality was still with her. Britt had deliberately evaded her comments about them doing things together.

She had fallen into the very trap she wanted most desperately to avoid—the one where she cared too much for Britt. She had let her most-carefully guarded emotions loose, and they had found Britt Carlton. Her first impression of him had probably been correct. He would never be content to settle down with one woman, to marry and raise a family. He would never allow himself to fall in love. He obviously wanted to be as free as the birds...to fly and soar where the winds took him.

She put her arm around his waist as he drew her closer to him. She had not meant for it to happen. She had not *wanted* it to happen. But it had. She had fallen in love with another charming scoundrel. She loved him so much. She did not know what she would do if he did not love her in return.

They had a late lunch before returning to Victoria. Britt had made reservations on the six o'clock ferry. As the catamaran moved through the water toward Seattle, each of them seemed to be lost in personal thoughts. It was Britt who broke the silence. ''You've been very quiet. Is everything okay?'' It was happening. He could feel it in his gut. She was pulling away from him. He had to do something, but what?

She offered him a weak smile. ''Yes, everything is fine.

I'm just a little tired, that's all. It's been a very busy weekend.''

When they arrived at the apartment building, Britt walked her to her door, unlocked it and placed her suitcase inside. He wrapped his arms around her and held her close, gently stroking her hair as he spoke. "Ashley, what's wrong? You've been different since yesterday. Have I done something to upset you?" He paused, again searching her eyes for some kind of truth, an answer to his dilemma. Perhaps it was more than just his fears run amok. She really was growing tired of him. It was an idea that left him deeply shaken. Even though it was a thought that had been uppermost in his mind all day, he still had not resolved the dilemma of what to do about it. An added sense of urgency crept into his voice. "Please, Ashley, talk to me. Tell me what's troubling you."

She returned his look, her eyes also searching for some type of truth and understanding. Her voice quavered as she finally forced out the difficult words. "What's the future for us, Britt? Where do we go from here?"

His worst fear had just become reality. She wanted out. His insides twisted into knots as he forced himself to say something—anything—that would put an end to the ominous silence that hung over them. He did not like the tenuous sound his voice projected. "I have a flight tomorrow morning and won't be back until Tuesday evening. Why don't we discuss this after I get back?"

He desperately needed to stall for time, to figure out what to do and what to say. He did not want to lose her. She meant too much to him, but making a commitment terrified him. There had to be some sort of solution, and he needed to figure out what it was. He had to handle it very carefully and not say the wrong thing. He had to stop her from breaking things off. He had to prevent her from leaving him.

Her entire existence crashed around her. She had never felt as miserable as she did at that moment. Her deepest fears spoke to her. He was putting her off. He was going to tell her that it had been fun, but that was all it would ever be. "Sure…maybe that would be better." She paused, hoping he would say something, but there was only silence.

"Good night, Britt." She turned and went into her apartment, closing and locking the door behind her.

She got ready for bed, climbed under the covers and turned out the light. A myriad of questions and concerns played through her mind. Did he at least care for her as much as he had for Joan? Had he been so deeply hurt that he would never allow himself to love again?

And then the worst thought of all: had they reached the limit of their relationship? Was this all it would ever be?

10

Ashley lay in bed the next morning with a headache and a sinking feeling in the pit of her stomach. She had been awake for two hours following an uneasy night's sleep. How was it possible for everything to be unraveling like this? How could she keep from losing Britt? She finally forced herself out of bed and prepared for work.

It was a very busy day at the office. She and Stu made the last-minute revisions to the reports he needed for his meetings. She was thankful for the heavy workload. It left no time for her personal concerns.

That evening she fell into a deep sleep, more from emotional exhaustion than from hard work.

The next day passed uneventfully, at least as far as her job was concerned. Home was another matter. She pulled into the parking garage at the apartment building just as Britt got out of his car and disappeared up the stairs. She got to the lobby mailboxes just as he disappeared down the walkway toward his apartment. Had he seen her? Was he purposely avoiding her? She didn't know and it was tearing her up inside.

She knocked at his apartment door. Perhaps a friendly offer of a glass of wine would help break the awkwardness that seemed to have materialized for no apparent reason.

"Ashley…" He appeared surprised to see her. He stood at the door without inviting her in. "Is there a problem?"

His voice sounded so cold to her, and he acted so distant. "A problem?" She mustered her courage and plunged forward. "No, there's no problem. I thought maybe you'd like to come over for a glass of wine…if you're not too busy. I think we have a few things we need to talk about." She offered an encouraging smile.

"I…uh…have been giving this some thought." His voice was reserved, his manner very nervous as he continued to block her entrance into his apartment. "In fact, I've been giving it a lot of thought. I…I think maybe we've been spending too much time together. Perhaps a little breather would be good for both of us…give us a chance to figure out where we are and where we want to go."

She felt as if she had been punched in the stomach. All the breath went out of her body to be replaced by a horribly sick feeling. "A breather?" She tried her best to pull herself together. The last thing she wanted to do was show him how much his words hurt. She squared her shoulders and set her jaw in determination. "Yes…well, I think you're right. Maybe it would be better if we saw other people."

Britt watched in silence as she turned and walked away from him. His heart sank; it felt as if a lead weight were tied to it. He knew she'd started growing distant while they were in Victoria, but he had not been prepared for what had just happened. His plan had been to start pulling away gradually, so that it would be less painful, so that her leaving would not throw him into a tailspin. Then she had hit him with his worst fear. She had already found someone else. He wanted to go after her and pull her into his arms, but she had made it very clear that it was too late.

He was as confused about his feelings as he was afraid of what they meant. He tried to convince himself that it was only a physical attraction that had gotten a little out of hand, nothing more. He knew he had to steel himself against his emotions. He could not allow himself to be in love with Ashley Thornton in spite of the fact that she had definitely worked her way into his heart. And he feared it was a place she would occupy forever. He had allowed himself to become vulnerable and once again it had slapped him in the face.

He had a flight early the next morning and would be gone for two days. He welcomed the time away. Perhaps it would clear his head and allow him to regain some sort of clear perspective and a bit of control over his life—or at least the emotional side of his life. He had been through an upheaval four years ago and did not know if he would be able to handle it again.

Ashley moved mechanically through Wednesday's workload. Stu's meetings had been very productive, the project all but completed. She had some reports to finish, then she would be able to call it a day. She was anxious to get home. She needed a quiet place to think, to try to make sense of things.

She felt drained as she walked slowly from the parking garage to her apartment, stopping to pick up her mail from the lobby box. It had been two days since she'd seen Britt. She had never felt as miserable as she did at that moment. She wondered if there was a special place where people could be put in some sort of suspended animation and then be revived when a way had been invented to mend a broken heart.

Her eyes started to mist over. She had known he was wrong for her, that he couldn't make a commitment and would eventually leave her. She had entered into the relationship with her eyes wide open, and everything she knew to be true had come to fruition. She also knew she would never love anyone the way she loved Britt Carlton.

The doorbell intruded into her misery. She opened the door and found a deliveryman with a package for her. After she signed for it, she took it into her living room and opened it. She was stunned to see a note from Jerry Broderick and a small velvet box containing the diamond ring she had returned to him when she'd broken their engagement.

She scanned the note, then went back and read it slowly and carefully. It said that he was very glad they had gotten a chance to talk while she was in Wichita. He wanted her to have the ring with no strings attached. He would never be able to give her ring to another woman, and he thought she deserved to keep it for all the hurt he had caused her.

She took the ring from the box. It was a very gracious gesture on his part, but she couldn't keep it. It would not be right. She dialed Jerry's number. She would thank him and tell him she would be returning the ring.

Britt had been pacing up and down his living room, impatiently waiting for Ashley to come home. They had to talk. He had been beyond miserable for the past two days. He had been too devastated to even think straight. He wasn't sure exactly how everything had gotten so totally messed up. He thought they were happy together, enjoying things just as they were. Then suddenly in Victoria she seemed to become distant, almost as if she were pulling away from him. Then when she asked him where their relationship was headed, all he could think of was that she wanted out.

He had taken the first step. By telling her they should take a breather, he thought he was protecting himself against the pain he knew would consume him if she told him goodbye. Instead of merely agreeing with him, she had added that they should see other people. He hadn't known what to say or how to respond. Had she already found someone else?

The one thing he did know was that somehow he needed to straighten out the problem before it caused a chasm so deep neither of them would ever be able to bridge it again. He tried to control his feelings of anxiety and foreboding.

After what seemed like hours, he saw the light finally go on in her apartment. He took a steadying breath to try to settle the mounting tension that churned in the pit of his stomach. He was a calm, rational man—levelheaded and cool in a crisis. So how could he have allowed his fears to take control as they had? He had actually told the woman he...*loved*—like it or not, there was no other way to put it—that he thought they were seeing too much of each other. He had done some stupid things in his life, but that one topped the list.

Then a horrible reality crashed through his consciousness. What if he had already lost her?

Britt hopped over the railing to her balcony. He looked through the sliding glass door. She was on the phone with someone. He could only catch snatches of her conversation, but it was enough for him to realize she was talking to her ex-fiancé. He saw her take a diamond ring from a box and put it on her finger. He heard her thanking him and saying it was a beautiful ring.

The pain that ripped through him was like nothing he

had ever before experienced. One thought remained above all else, blotting out any and all reality—it was Joan all over again. Only this time it was more than he could endure. He loved Ashley so very much. He had never told her, but that didn't make it any less real. His mind went blank as he tried to shut out his anguish. He managed to make it back to his own apartment, his actions directed from some inner place where he sought refuge against the overwhelming pain.

Ashley had seen Britt on her balcony. Unbridled joy welled inside her the moment she spotted him. He had come to talk things out. There was still a chance for them to work out their problems. Then she saw him leave without coming in. It puzzled her that he didn't say anything, but she assumed he would be right back. She finished her conversation with Jerry, then repackaged the ring so she could send it back to him.

She glanced toward the balcony. Her anticipation dropped a little when she didn't see any sign of Britt. She went to the kitchen, opened a bottle of wine and carried it to the living room along with two glasses. He had still not returned. While she waited, she went through the mail she had picked up on her way from the garage.

She glanced at the clock. Confusion clouded her thoughts. Why had he appeared on her balcony then disappeared without a word? A sick feeling churned in the pit of her stomach. Was it possible that he had overheard part of her phone conversation with Jerry? Had he misinterpreted the combination of the phone call and the fact that she was wearing the ring and admiring it?

Panic gripped her as she raced next door. A new fear took over as she insistently pushed his doorbell. There was no answer. She pounded on the door and called his name. Still no answer. She raced to the parking garage. Her heart sank and her eyes filled with tears. His car was gone.

She woke at eleven o'clock that night, still dressed in the same clothes she had put on that morning. Slowly she rose, rubbed her puffy red eyes and made her way through the darkened apartment to the bathroom. She undressed, put on her robe and looked at her reflection in the mirror. She didn't like what she saw: pain mixed with fear. She trudged listlessly back into the living room and plopped down on the couch. She sat unmoving, not seeing, not thinking...and trying not to feel.

At midnight Britt's apartment was still dark. She went to the kitchen and slowly opened a drawer. After a moment's hesitation, she removed the key he had given her so she could water his plants when he was gone. She debated a long time about using it, then finally shook away the doubts. After unlocking his door, she entered the darkened apartment.

She called his name only to be greeted by silence. Clicking on the lights, she looked around, then checked his bedroom. Drawers had been pulled out and clothes strewn around the room. He had obviously packed in a hurry and departed. She returned to her own apartment. Hopefully sleep would help ease the pain.

Ashley woke early the next morning, feeling as exhausted as she had when she went to bed. As soon as she arrived at her office, she called the charter company and talked to Ellen.

"I don't know where he's gone. He didn't come back to his apartment at all last night. Do you know where he is, Ellen? Have you heard from him?" A sob caught in her throat. "Is he okay?"

"I have no idea where he is," Ellen said, concern in her voice. "All I know is I came in this morning and found a note on my desk telling me to replace him on all his scheduled flights...indefinitely."

Ashley's voice bordered on hysterics. "What do you mean, *indefinitely?* How can he just take off like that and still keep his job?"

"He and his father own the company. Britt runs it."

"He *owns* the company?"

"Yes, didn't you know? This is the largest privately owned charter company in the Pacific Northwest."

"No...I didn't know..." Ashley's voice trailed off and her mind refused to put her thoughts in any type of order. "If you hear from him, let me know...please."

"Of course."

Ashley hung up the phone and sat quietly, her hand still resting on the receiver. She was on the verge of tears when Stu walked up behind her and put his arm comfortingly around her shoulder. "Would you like to talk about it?"

She looked up into his wise, understanding eyes. She could control her grief no longer. Through tears she told him the whole story. "And now he's disappeared. No one knows where he's gone." She looked again into Stu's sympathetic face. "He must think I've gone back with Jerry, that I've been leading him on, lying to him just like his ex-fiancée did."

Stu squeezed her shoulder reassuringly. "Perhaps this is for the best. I've known Britt for a while. He's a terrific pilot, very likable, but—well, I didn't want to say anything earlier because it was none of my business. I've seen how he is with women and relationships, and I can't say I'm surprised by his actions. I know this is very painful for you, but maybe it's better that it end now rather than later when you've become even more involved."

He handed her his handkerchief to dry her eyes. "We're ahead of schedule on our project. I think you should take a few days off, maybe go visit your family." His expression brightened. "Call the travel agency right now and have them charge a plane ticket to the company. In fact, I don't even want to see you back here until—" he paused a moment to think "—until next Wednesday. That's a week."

"Oh, thank you, Stu. You're a wonderful man. Your wife and children are lucky people to have you." She jumped up from her chair and gave him a warm hug of appreciation.

"Now get out of here before you have me believing all those nice things. Scat!"

She left the office and drove straight home. When she entered her apartment, an oppressive sense of loss settled over her. Britt was gone, no one knew where. She might never see him again. She sank into the couch, her despair sinking even lower. She stayed in her apartment the rest of that day, and the next day. On Friday afternoon when he still had not returned, she finally called the travel agency and made a plane reservation for Saturday morning.

Ashley spotted her mother, father and brother as soon as she stepped out of the jetway at the Wichita airport. She ran to them, throwing her arms around all of them at once.

When they arrived at her parents' house, Bobby carried her suitcase to her room, then went to the patio to join the family. Ashley sat at the table, trying to pretend that nothing was wrong—and doing a very poor job of it. Finally she stood up and headed for the kitchen door. "I'm kind of tired. I haven't had much sleep lately. I think I'll take a little nap."

After Ashley was out of sight, Marilyn turned to her husband. "She's hurting so much. I wish there was something we could do."

Mike patted her hand. "I know, but we really can't interfere. We can give her our love and support, but we can't make her decisions for her. This is something between Ashley and Britt. It's for them to work out."

Bobby, who had been silently listening to everything, finally spoke up. "I like Britt. I was kind of looking forward to having him as a brother-in-law. What do you think really happened?"

Marilyn reached over and brushed an errant lock of hair from her son's forehead. "From what Ashley was saying, it sounds to me like there was some sort of misunderstanding, and now Britt has taken off and no one seems to know where he is."

Mike stood up. He made an effort to be objective. "Well, I think you'd have to be blind not to notice how much he adored her when they were here. His feelings couldn't have changed that much in a couple of weeks."

The rest of the afternoon faded into evening without Ashley making an appearance from her bedroom. Finally Marilyn went to check on her. "Ashley, dear, it's six o'clock. It's almost time for dinner." Marilyn gently shook her shoulder, trying to wake her from her nap. "Come on, dear. If you don't get up now, you won't be able to sleep tonight."

Ashley opened her eyes then mumbled, "Okay, Mother. I'm getting up. I'll be out in a few minutes."

Marilyn left the room, closing the door behind her. Ashley rolled over onto her back, pulled the covers up around her shoulders and closed her eyes. She made no effort to get out of bed.

She tried to figure things out logically. She could understand how Britt could be very hurt by what he thought he'd seen and heard. After all, she hadn't told him about running into Jerry at the grocery store and their ensuing conversation. Her emotions, however, refused to let her believe that was the case. Why had he not waited for an explanation? Surely his heart must have known the truth, must have told him how much she loved him.

She fingered the gold bracelet that had not been off her wrist since Britt had given it to her for her birthday. Perhaps she could derive some sort of comfort from it.

A while later Ashley finally made an appearance for dinner. She sat at her old place at the table but only played at eating, pushing the food around her plate without really putting any of it in her mouth. After a while, she shoved the plate away. "I'm sorry, Mother. I guess I'm just not very hungry." She left the table and went to her room, closing the door behind her.

Ashley rose very early the next morning, grabbed a cup of coffee and went out on the patio to watch the sunrise. The early-morning sky held just a hint of red on the eastern horizon. The color quickly changed to pink, then gold, and finally to blue as she slowly sipped her coffee. She knew she couldn't continue to hide from her pain and turmoil by sequestering herself in the childhood safety of her parents' home. She had a job and a new home of her own in Seattle. She needed to get on with her life.

"Hi-ya, sis. You're up early." Bobby sat down at the table with his cup of coffee. "Is that all you're having for breakfast?"

She looked at the cup of coffee and then looked at Bobby. She could see his concern. A warm smile spread across her face as she reached out and gently patted his cheek. "No, it's not." She headed toward the kitchen door. "I'm cooking. What would you like?"

Bobby followed her back into the kitchen, obviously relieved at her lifted spirits. "You know me, I'll eat anything. I'll take whatever you're fixing."

Her mood seemed much better, her painful inner turmoil somehow lightened. Her family gave a collective sigh of relief, but continued to carefully avoid the subject of Britt and what had happened between the two of them. The day passed quickly. Sunset found them sitting on the patio with Mike lighting the charcoal in preparation for cooking steaks.

"I'm going back to Seattle tomorrow morning. I need to get back to work." Ashley's statement was made in a newly confident tone of voice, her manner reaffirming her decision to get on with her life. Marilyn and Mike exchanged knowing looks, obviously pleased that she had taken matters firmly in hand and made the right decision.

By midnight the house was dark with everyone asleep. The solitude was broken by the intrusion of the doorbell, then someone banging loudly at the door. Mike came out of his bedroom and met Bobby in the hall.

"I'll get it, Dad." Bobby flipped on the porch light and yanked open the door. "Do you have any idea what time it is…" His angry words trailed off as he focused on Britt standing on the porch.

The two men stared at each other, then Britt spoke. "Where is she? I want to see her—now." He opened the screen door and stepped inside without waiting to be invited.

Bobby stepped in front of him, blocking his path. "Hold it. I don't know what you did to her, but when she arrived here she was in a pretty bad emotional state. She's better now, but I'm going to be real unhappy if you do anything that puts her back in that condition.'' Bobby fixed Britt with an intense stare. His six feet, four inch height and football player's bulk seemed to loom over Britt. ''Do I make myself clear?''

Britt's voice was flat, conveying no expression at all. He stretched his own six-one height and stared back at Bobby. ''I've had precious little sleep over the past few days. My gut is turned inside out. I'm in no mood for this. Now where is she?''

Bobby considered the situation for a moment, then stepped aside. ''The second door on the right.''

Britt walked swiftly down the hall. As he reached Ashley's door, he saw Mike standing by his bedroom door. He nodded tersely, acknowledging his presence. ''Mike.'' He entered Ashley's room, closing the door quietly behind him.

Bobby walked up to his dad, a broad smile on his face. ''Looks like hell, doesn't he? I'd say he's been suffering through just as much turmoil as Ashley.''

Mike placed his hand on Bobby's shoulder and returned his smile. ''I believe you're right, son. I believe you're right. Now I think we should all go back to our rooms and let Ashley and Britt deal with this by themselves.''

Mike went back to his bedroom and sat on the edge of the bed next to Marilyn. ''Well, dear...I believe I won our little bet. I said he'd come for her before morning.''

Britt stood at the side of Ashley's bed, gazing lovingly at her peaceful face. He grabbed her suitcase and quickly packed her things, then picked up her robe from the foot of the bed. ''Ashley.'' He gently shook her shoulder. ''Wake up. We're going home.''

Slowly she opened her eyes and tried to focus on Britt,

but she was having difficulty discerning the difference between the reality of his presence and the fantasy of her dream. "Britt?" She reached out her hand and touched his whisker-stubbled face. "Is that really you?"

He pulled her into a sitting position and helped her on with her robe. "Shh...we can talk when we get home. I have a cab waiting in the driveway. The plane is being refueled so we can take off right away."

Her voice still held a husky edge of sleep. "I can't just leave. Mother and Daddy will wonder where I've gone."

"No they won't. They know I'm here. You can call them when we get home." He helped her with her slippers, then scooped her up in his arms and carried her down the hall.

He paused when he saw Bobby staring out the door at the cab. "Would you grab Ashley's bag from her room?"

Bobby turned around to find Britt standing behind him with Ashley snuggled in his arms, her head resting on his shoulder. He managed a little grin. "Well, she looks like she's going willingly." He held Britt's look for a quick moment, then said, "Take good care of her," as he went to get her bag.

Britt answered softly, his love for Ashley reflected in every breath he took. "I will."

11

Britt placed Ashley in the middle of his bed. She had dropped off to sleep again. He was tired, too. In fact, he was bone weary. It was only the strange working of a pure adrenaline surge that had kept him going the past few hours.

He stared at Ashley sleeping peacefully in his bed. His gaze lovingly traced each of her delicate features. She was the only one in his life, the only woman who would ever have his heart totally and completely. His intention had been to talk to her as soon as she got home from work that Wednesday evening, to try to explain the deep-seated fears that had caused him to act the way he had—and to ask her forgiveness for behaving like a damned fool.

Then the bottom had dropped out of his life when he'd overheard her on the phone talking to the man she had told him was her *ex*-fiancé while admiring the engagement ring on her finger. He had stumbled off in a blinding cloud of despair and rejection and the worst pain of his entire life. He was not even sure of the exact order of events that followed. He knew he had thrown some clothes into a bag and started driving. He remembered crossing the border into Canada. He had managed a couple of hours sleep in his car at a roadside rest somewhere—he was not sure exactly where. All he'd wanted to do was numb the unbearable pain that pounded inside him.

It was early Sunday afternoon when he had finally come to his senses and returned home. He went directly to her apartment before even going to his own, but she wasn't there. He saw Shirley on her way to the parking garage. She told him that Ashley had left Saturday morning for Wichita. Total panic instantly claimed him. He raced to the airport. It had been late Sunday night when he touched down at the Cessna company airstrip on the west side of town and called for a taxi.

Britt continued to watch Ashley as she slept. What he had thought of as being the most difficult part of his task had now been completed. He had gotten her back to Seattle, to his apartment, to his bed. He'd been prepared for a really tough time with her family. Instead they'd handed her over to him—no questions, no problems. It was almost as if they had been expecting him.

He stretched out next to her. Every fiber of his body ached. They would talk this out in the morning. Right now he was much too exhausted to deal with anything else. He wrapped his arms around her, drawing her to him. He kissed her softly on the cheek and whispered, "I love you." Almost before the words were out of his mouth, he, too, had fallen asleep.

Ashley lay quietly in Britt's bed, not wanting to wake him. She watched as he drew slow, even breaths, sleeping peacefully. The stress and tension of the past few days still showed on his handsome face, even with his features relaxed in sleep. He had not even bothered to get undressed; he still wore the same clothes he'd had on when he carried her from her parents' house.

She remained in his bed for almost an hour after she

woke. Her mind went over the events of the past few days
as she tried to straighten things out and make sense of
what had happened.

She watched Britt for a moment longer as he slept, then
quietly slipped out of his bed, collected her belongings
and went next door to her own apartment. After taking a
shower and dressing, she stepped out onto her balcony
with her cup of coffee and sat down to think.

Three more hours passed before Britt rolled over,
slowly opened his eyes and tried to clear the fuzziness
from his head. He reached for the clock, then jerked to
an upright position as the numbers came into focus. It was
noon. He instantly became aware of the ominous silence
that filled the apartment. He jumped out of bed and raced
to the living room. She was gone.

Ashley heard the sound of Britt's sliding door, which
startled her back to reality. As soon as he stepped out
onto his balcony, she saw the panic and frantic urgency
on his face. Then when he saw her, his features softened,
and he let out a sigh of relief.

He walked to the edge of the balcony, placed his hands
on the railing and leaned forward. "There you are." He
tried to smile, but the best he could manage was a slight
tug at the corners of his mouth. "When I woke up, I
couldn't find you. I didn't know where you'd gone. I was
afraid—" His confusion and hurt were visible in the silvery depths of his eyes. "Ashley...please don't go away.
I'll be right back. I have to get cleaned up. I don't remember when I last shaved, and I've been wearing the
same clothes for over twenty-four hours straight."

He looked at her again, then quickly hopped up on the
railing and crossed to her balcony. He knelt down in front
of her chair and cupped her face in his hands. "We can
work everything out." He leaned forward and kissed her

lightly on the lips, then wrapped his arms around her and held her as he stroked her hair.

She melted into his embrace. It felt so good to have his arms around her again. He was right, they would work out their problems. Everything would be okay—it just had to be. She spoke his name in a soft whisper. "Britt...I..." Her voice faltered as she experienced too much emotion to continue. The words would not come out.

He held her head against his shoulder and gently rocked her in his arms. "We'll talk this out in a few minutes. I'll be right back." After a moment he released her and started toward the balcony railing, then turned toward her again, his voice filled with pain and hurt. "Please tell me you're not going anywhere, that you'll still be here when I return."

"I won't go anywhere," she answered softly. She watched in silence as he hopped back over the railing and disappeared into his own apartment. She remained in the chair, unable to move. Her emotions were on a roller coaster. There were so many questions without answers. She was so confused...and so fearful of losing him.

She continued to sit on her balcony as she watched dark storm clouds gathering on the horizon. The forecast had said rain that afternoon, extending through the night and into the next day. She wondered for a moment if the storm clouds were an omen, a portent of things to come, but she quickly dismissed the unwelcome thought. Nervousness and anxiety churned in the pit of her stomach as she waited for Britt to return, not at all sure about what was going to happen next.

He quickly showered, shaved and pulled on some clean clothes. He didn't want to be gone from her one minute longer than was absolutely necessary. His center of reality had turned to chaos. All he knew for certain was that he loved her with all his heart and would do whatever he had to do to keep from losing her.

Fifteen minutes passed before he reappeared on his balcony. He was dressed in sweatpants and sweatshirt, was clean shaven with his hair tousled from the quick towel drying. His face still looked a little drawn and haggard, but most of the deep tension and stress lines were gone. He quickly hopped across the railing and sat down in the other chair next to her.

He took her hand in his, laced their fingers together and sat in silence trying to gather his thoughts, trying to determine the best way to proceed. He held her hand tightly, afraid to let go—afraid if he did she would float away from him much like a balloon on a string.

He cleared his throat and took another calming breath, then started to speak, his words coming nonstop. He feared that if he paused before he'd said everything he wouldn't be able to go on.

"What happened here, Ashley? What happened to us? I thought we were happy together, enjoying our relationship just the way it was. Then suddenly in Victoria you seemed to become distant, to pull away from me."

He continued to speak, his anxiety mounting with each word. "All I could think of was that you were growing tired of me. I knew at that moment I was in so deep that I wouldn't be able to handle losing you. The only solution I could think of was to try to ease myself out of the situation. I thought if I started distancing myself from you by suggesting that we slow things down a bit, it would make the inevitable easier."

He brushed his fingertips across her cheek. His words had an almost-desolate quality about them. "But the only thing I accomplished was to make myself miserable. And then the final blow came when you told me you thought we should see other people. That triggered my worst fear, that you had already found someone else.''

A shudder darted through his body. He leaned forward and tentatively took her face in his trembling hands. He searched her eyes for some type of sign, some clue. ''Then I overheard you talking on the phone to Jerry while admiring the diamond ring on your finger. There was no animosity in your voice, nothing about your manner that suggested there was anything amiss between you and the man you said had cheated on you while you were engaged. You certainly didn't look or sound like a woman confronting a man who had betrayed her.''

She could see the hurt and pain in his eyes and heard it in his voice. A small flame began to flicker and grow inside her as she realized he was not terminating their relationship, but trying to save it. She placed her hands on top of his. She could feel him trembling—at least, she thought it was him. It might have been her.

The dark storm clouds hung lower and lower in the sky, cutting off the afternoon light. The wind picked up. A gust blew across the balcony. Neither Ashley nor Britt allowed it to intrude into the situation that absorbed them.

''Didn't it occur to you to stick around long enough to ask?'' Her words were tentative. She didn't want to sound argumentative or too harsh.

''Yes, you're right. That's what I should have done. But all I could think of, all I could see, was that you were going to leave me and marry an old boyfriend. It was Joan all over again. Only this time it was a million times more devastating—more than I could bear.''

She glanced down at the floor as she paused to gather her thoughts, then looked up to recapture his gaze. ''When we first met, I told myself that you were the type who would never be tied down to one woman. I firmly believed that you were just like Jerry—a flagrant womanizer who was only out for a good time without any hint of a true commitment. I told myself that as long as we were only friends, I could enjoy our fun times together but it could never be anything serious. I'd been hurt by that type of man before, and I couldn't allow it to happen again.

"Then, as time went on, I managed to convince myself that maybe I had been wrong...that maybe I had a chance of being that one woman. But when we returned from Victoria and I asked you what our future was—well, you sidestepped my question and put me off. All I could think of was that I had been right all along, that you could never be satisfied with only one woman in a committed relationship and that you were tired of me and were looking for a way out. I didn't mean to push you into something you didn't want, to make you feel trapped. I just needed to know if there was any future for us."

He grabbed her by the shoulders and stared intently into her eyes. "I admit that you scared the hell out of me. All of a sudden you were talking about the future, where our relationship was going. I was happy with things just the way they were, then suddenly you were talking about matters I didn't want to think about or deal with. I needed to buy some time so I could think of what to do...." His voice trailed off as his certainty started to fade. "Or at least I thought that was what I needed to do."

Large drops began to hit the balcony as it started raining. A cold wind hit against them, the rain stinging their skin. They ignored the discomfort as he pulled her to her feet and enfolded her in his arms. He held her tightly against his body. She began to shiver, partly from the cold and partly from the emotional release of the turmoil that had been trapped inside her.

The rain pounded down in sheets, soaking everything

in sight. He moved her toward the open balcony door. "Come on, let's get inside. We're going to be drenched if we stay out here." They hurried into her apartment, closing the sliding door behind them.

He enfolded her in his arms, holding her close against his body as she rested her head on his chest. In a tentative voice she asked him the final unanswered question. "Why did you disappear like that? I waited and waited but you never came home. I thought I was going to die. Stu told me to take a few days off. I finally flew to Wichita Saturday morning." She looked up at his face, her eyes questioning. "Why did you disappear?"

"Why?" A hint of pain still lingered in his eyes as he answered her. "Because I'm a damned fool, that's why. I didn't even know what I was doing. I wandered around in a daze, barely functioning. All I could think of was that I had lost you, that you would be gone from my life for good. It was Saturday night when I finally came to my senses and Sunday before I got home. When I found you had gone to Wichita...well, all I could think of was that you were going to marry another man. I knew I had to do everything in my power to stop you."

A loud clap of thunder rattled the rain-spattered windows. He held her closer as they stood together just inside the balcony door. "I'm so sorry, Ashley. Can you ever forgive me?"

"Only if you can forgive me."

"Do you think we could begin again, as if the past few days had never happened?" Britt turned her so they were looking out the rain-streaked balcony door. "Just like this rain...everything will be washed clean, everything will be sparkling new and shiny."

He drew her to him again as he lowered his mouth to hers, his hands caressing her back. They both felt the fires of passion build between them. Their clothes tumbled to the floor as they succumbed to their heated desires. Their bodies entwined as they reveled in the enticing sensations. As the heat of their passion reached a fever pitch, he held her tightly and cried out, "I love you, Ashley."

His words reverberated through her mind, and her spirits sailed on his cries of love, bringing her happiness beyond anything she had ever known. She wrapped herself tightly around him as she softly murmured in his ear, "I love you, too."

He tightened his embrace and whispered the words over and over. "I love you, Ashley. I love you. I love you. I've wanted to tell you that, but couldn't get the words out. I love you."

The rain continued to pelt the windowpanes as afternoon drifted into evening. They held each other close, neither speaking. Each was lost in the magical moments of their quiet togetherness. He stroked her glossy hair, nuzzled her neck and kissed her cheek as she caressed his taut shoulders and back. She slowly rubbed her bare leg against his. They were bound together on all levels of their existence.

Britt was the one who finally interrupted their silent reverie. "Ashley, honey..." He paused, his words catching in his throat from the overwhelming emotions of the moment. He tried again to speak. "Did you mean it...when you said you loved me? Did you really mean it?" He held his breath as he waited for her to answer.

She kissed his cheek then murmured in his ear, "Of course I meant it." She snuggled in his arms, getting as close to him as she could. The full length of her body pressed against his. Her voice was soft and slightly husky. "I love you very much."

His lips nibbled at the corner of her mouth. "Do you have to go to work tomorrow?"

"Mmm…" Her eyes closed as the sensations of his touch drifted across her skin. "What is tomorrow… Tuesday? No, Stu let me off until Wednesday." She lifted her face to his, seductively drew his lower lip into the moist warmth of her mouth, held it there for a second then released it. "Why?"

He nuzzled her neck. "Good." He slowly covered her face with soft, sensual kisses. "I have some plans for us for tomorrow." His hand slowly stroked the length of her body, his fingertips titillating her senses as they skimmed over her bare skin.

Her body responded instantly to his touch. Her breathing grew faster, her heart pounded, and her pulse raced. Her voice filled with emotion as she forced out the words. "What kind of plans?"

"You'll see tomorrow." He recaptured her mouth, tasting her lips, savoring her sweetness.

Sometime during the night the rain stopped and the clouds drifted away. The sunrise painted the sky with all its brilliant colors. Ashley lay awake snuggled next to Britt, wrapped in the warm security of his arms. She still floated on the euphoric high from the night before. He loved her, nothing else mattered. They had shared that love—the emotional as well as the physical.

And after they made love, they had talked. All the fears and hidden secrets were shared, all the concerns and anxieties brought out into the open and discussed. They had fallen asleep secure in the knowledge that they had grown even closer.

Britt had been awake for a little while, but had not moved for fear of disturbing her sleep. He looked at her peaceful face, her long lashes resting against the top of her cheek. His heart swelled with the overwhelming feelings of love that coursed through his veins. He had never felt as complete as he did at that moment, as he did whenever he was near her. She gave his life a purpose and meaning that it had never had before.

Ashley slowly rolled over in Britt's arms, her silky skin brushing tantalizingly against his body. She opened her eyes and focused on him. A smile came to her lips as she softly purred in his ear, "Good morning. Have you been awake long?"

"Not long." His fingertips traced the outline of her mouth and moved along her jaw then down her neck. "Did you sleep well?"

She snuggled closer to him, rubbing her leg against his. She closed her eyes as she savored the sensations of his touch. She felt his hand glide smoothly down her back, along her hip and seductively across her bare bottom. "I had a marvelous night's sleep. I feel totally rested, alive, ready to face whatever comes my way."

He abruptly sat up in bed. "Good!" He threw off the covers, reached over and gave her a teasing little slap on the rear end.

"Britt!" Her shocked expression matched her tone of voice. She immediately put her hands protectively across her bottom. "What are you up to?"

He leaned forward and quickly captured her nipple in his mouth, his tongue teasing it to a taut peak. After a moment he released the delicate peak, looked up at her face and grinned. Cupping her other breast in his hand he said, "I'm up to about here."

She laughed, an open, easy laugh. She enjoyed his teasing and his unpredictable antics. "What's gotten into you this morning?"

He cocked his head to one side and raised an eyebrow, his impish grin in place. "It's not what's gotten into me, it's what I've gotten into..." His voice trailed off as his expression turned serious.

He took her hand in his and climbed out of bed, pulling her with him. He wrapped his arms around her and looked into the depths of her turquoise eyes. He saw all his love reflected and returned. "Have I told you lately just how very much I love you?"

She rested her head against his chest as she spoke softly, "Not today you haven't."

"I don't want to wear out the words, say them so much that they no longer have any meaning. If I keep it to only a hundred times a day, would that be okay?"

"You could never say it too much. I'll never get tired of hearing those words."

"I love you, Ashley. I love you so much that it still frightens me." He held her close to him for a moment then released her. "Come on, I'll race you to the shower." He grinned mischievously. "I'll let you wash my back if I can wash your front."

She seemed surprised as she looked at him questioningly. "The way you were carrying on, I was sure we would be spending the entire day in bed."

"There isn't anything I'd rather do than spend the day in bed with you—except for one thing," he said, his eyes sparkling.

She peered into their silvery depths. All the emotions he felt for her were there for the world to see. Her voice became soft as she whispered, not knowing where her question would lead. "What is that one thing?"

He answered softly, "You'll see." He kissed her tenderly on the lips. His mood instantly changed to a casual, upbeat manner, his voice full of enthusiasm. "As much fun as standing in a warm shower and rubbing soapy lather all over each other would be, for the sake of time I think we should part company for the moment. I'll be back to pick you up in about an hour and a half.''

She looked at him quizzically. ''I don't suppose you'd like to tell me what you have on your mind?''

He grinned at her as he tickled his fingertips over the soft skin of her cheek. ''Not yet.'' He grabbed his clothes from the floor, quickly dressed and left her apartment.

Britt landed the jet at the South Lake Tahoe airport. He said nothing as he grabbed her hand and led her off the plane and to a waiting rental car. They drove through town and across the state line from the California side to the Nevada side of the lake.

He made a left-hand turn off the main highway and headed down toward the water and a secluded stretch of shoreline. Pulling the car into a parking lot adjacent to a small building, he turned off the engine. He helped her out of the car, put his arm around her shoulder and walked with her down to the edge of the lake, stopping by a large rock at the shoreline.

''It's so beautiful here, Britt—the mountains ringing the lake, the crystal-clear water, the crisp air with the scent of pine trees. This is such a lovely setting. Everything is so perfect.''

''Not perfect...not quite yet.'' He put his hand into his pocket and withdrew a small velvet bag. He untied the delicate gold cord that held the bag closed and took out a ring—an exquisite gold setting with a double row of small flawless diamonds.

Little tremors of excitement darted through her body. She stared at the ring then looked up at him. She was afraid to even think about what was happening.

He leaned forward and lightly brushed his lips against hers before speaking. "Ten years ago, on my parents' twenty-fifth wedding anniversary, my father bought my mother a new ring. My mother gave me her old ring. Her only request was that I save it until I found someone special, someone to whom I could give it along with my love and heart. It's been in the safe at the office ever since that day. There wasn't anyone worthy of having this ring... until I met you."

"No one? Not even—"

"No. It never occurred to me to give it to Joan."

He looked deeply into her eyes as he knelt on the ground next to where she was seated on the rock. "I want you to have it."

A shiver moved through her body as the full magnitude of what he was saying finally hit her. Her eyes misted over. "Britt? Is this...are you asking—" Emotion choked off the words.

He looked out over the sparkling blue water of the lake as he took a steadying breath and gathered his words. "Ashley, I love you very much. Would you do me the honor of marrying me?"

The tears that had been welling in her eyes burst over the rims and rolled down her cheeks. Her unbounded joy bubbled over. "You're asking me to marry you?" She threw her arms around his neck. "Yes! Yes! Yes! Of course I'll marry you."

"Would right now be a good time?"

A look of confusion darted across her face, and her tone became hesitant. "Now? Do you mean *right* now?"

He stroked her hair as he brushed his lips softly across her mouth. "Yes, right now." He stood and drew her within his embrace, then reached out his arm indicating the small building at the other end of the parking lot. "That is a wedding chapel."

"Britt...I...this is all so sudden. I always thought that when I married, my family would be there, my father would give me away—the traditional formal wedding. You know, all the trimmings."

He felt a rising sense of panic. He took a couple of calming breaths. "Ashley, honey...we can have whatever kind of wedding ceremony you want. We can invite anyone you want, we'll have it where you want and when you want—as a second ceremony." He took the ring, placed it in her palm and closed her fingers around it. "However, before you can change your mind..." The emotion of the moment choked his words. He leaned forward and kissed her tenderly on the lips then looked into her eyes. "If you don't marry me right now, I think I'll just die."

She opened her hand and looked at the exquisite gold and diamond ring and then at Britt. She smiled lovingly as she answered him, "Never let it be said that I didn't do all I could to save another human life."

Britt took Ashley's hand in his and led her across the parking lot to the wedding chapel. As he opened the door for her, he whispered in her ear, "Now everything is perfect."

* * * * * *

Take 4 bestselling love stories FREE

Plus get a FREE surprise gift!

Special Limited-time Offer

Mail to Silhouette Reader Service™

> 3010 Walden Avenue
> P.O. Box 1867
> Buffalo, N.Y. 14269-1867

YES! Please send me 4 free Silhouette Yours Truly™ novels and my free surprise gift. Then send me 4 brand-new novels every other month, which I will receive months before they appear in bookstores. Bill me at the low price of $2.90 each plus 25¢ delivery and applicable sales tax, if any.* That's the complete price and a savings of over 10% off the cover prices—quite a bargain! I understand that accepting the books and gift places me under no obligation ever to buy any books. I can always return a shipment and cancel at any time. Even if I never buy another book from Silhouette, the 4 free books and the surprise gift are mine to keep forever.

201 SEN CF2X

Name	(PLEASE PRINT)	
Address	Apt. No.	
City	State	Zip

This offer is limited to one order per household and not valid to present Silhouette Yours Truly™ subscribers. *Terms and prices are subject to change without notice. Sales tax applicable in N.Y.

USYRT-296

©1996 Harlequin Enterprises Limited

SILHOUETTE YOURS TRULY™

invites you to patronize

Weddings, Inc.

a delightful new miniseries by
Karen Templeton

Weddings, Inc.: Because wedding planning is a tricky business—but love makes it all worthwhile.

WEDDING DAZE

March 1998: As one of the best wedding planners in Atlanta, Brianna Fairchild knew the business inside and out—but what she didn't know was that she was about to become her own best customer!

WEDDING BELLE

July 1998: After three almost trips to the altar in as many years, pampered Southern belle Charlotte Westwood had no sooner sworn off hoping for a happily-ever-after than she met a most *un*likely prince.

And look for WEDDING? IMPOSSIBLE! coming soon— only in Silhouette Yours Truly.

Available at your favorite retail outlet.

MARILYN PAPPANO

Concludes the twelve-book series— 36 Hours—in June 1998 with the final installment

YOU MUST REMEMBER THIS

Who was "Martin Smith"? The sexy stranger had swept into town in the midst of catastrophe, with no name and no clue to his past. Shy, innocent Julie Crandall found herself fascinated—and willing to risk everything to be by his side. But as the shocking truth regarding his identity began to emerge, Julie couldn't help but wonder if the *real* man would prove simply too hot to handle.

For Martin and Julie and *all* the residents of Grand Springs, Colorado, the storm-induced blackout had been just the beginning of 36 Hours that changed *everything*—and guaranteed a lifetime forecast of happiness for twelve very special couples.

Available at your favorite retail outlet.

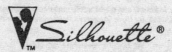

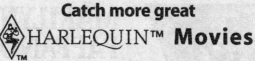

In **July 1998** comes

THE MACKENZIE FAMILY

by *New York Times* bestselling author

LINDA HOWARD

The dynasty continues with:

Mackenzie's Pleasure: Rescuing a pampered ambassador's daughter from her terrorist kidnappers was a piece of cake for navy SEAL Zane Mackenzie. It was only afterward, when they were alone together, that the real danger began....

Mackenzie's Magic: Talented trainer Maris Mackenzie was wanted for horse theft, but with no memory, she had little chance of proving her innocence or eluding the real villains. Her only hope for salvation? The stranger in her bed.

Available this July for the first time ever in a two-in-one trade-size edition. Fall in love with the Mackenzies for the first time—or all over again!

Available at your favorite retail outlet.

Silhouette Books